Mademoiselle Blanche

A Novel

by

John D. Barry

Double 9 BOOKS

Mademoiselle Blanche
A Novel
by John D. Barry

ISBN: 978-93-70814-84-4

Published by

DOUBLE 9 BOOKS
2/13-B, Ansari Road
Daryaganj, New Delhi – 110002
info@double9books.com
www.double9books.com
Tel. 011-40042856

ABOUT THE AUTHOR

John D. Barry was a writer, editor, and journalist known for his contributions to literature and social commentary during the late 19th and early 20th centuries. Barry pursued a career in journalism, becoming an influential voice in literary and cultural circles. His keen observations on human nature and society were reflected in both his fiction and non-fiction works.

Throughout his career, Barry wrote extensively on themes of ambition, morality, and personal introspection, often exploring the complexities of human relationships and societal expectations. He was known for his ability to blend psychological depth with engaging storytelling, offering readers both entertainment and thought-provoking insights. In addition to his literary pursuits, Barry contributed to periodicals and newspapers, where he provided commentary on contemporary social issues. His works captured the shifting dynamics of his time, particularly in relation to class, ambition, and cultural change. Barry's legacy endures through his contributions to literature and journalism, offering a window into the concerns and aspirations of his era.

CONTENTS

Chapter I

"André!"

"Yes, monsieur."

The little waiter, with anxiety in his smooth, blond face, hurried to the table.

"Bring me the *Soir*."

André shot away, and presently returned, paper in hand.

"What is there good at the theatres, André?"

André wiped his hands in his soiled apron, and looked thoughtful.

"There's the *Folies Bergères*, monsieur. Dumont sings to-night."

"Oh, she tires me. Her voice is cracked."

"There's Madame Judic at the *Variétés*," André suggested, tentatively.

"I saw her in the last piece."

André scratched his head, and stared at the figure at the table.

"Monsieur likes the *Cirque*, does he not?"

Monsieur did not look up from the paper. "What's at the *Cirque* now, André?"

"At the *Cirque Parisien*? There's Mademoiselle Blanche, the acrobat. They say she's a marvel, monsieur,—and beautiful,—the most beautiful woman in Paris. She dives from the top of the building backwards—hundreds of feet."

"So you think it's really good, André?"

André nodded. Monsieur dropped the paper, paid his bill, left a little fee for the *garçon*, and took himself off. At the entrance he stopped and surveyed the surging crowd in the *Boulevard Montmartre*. He had just finished an excellent dinner with a glass of *chartreuse verte*; so he felt particularly complacent. As he prodded his teeth with the easy grace of the Frenchman who knows no shame of the toothpick, he tried to think out a plan for the evening. Nothing better occurred to him than André's suggestion. He was not in the mood for the *Casino de Paris*, nor for any of the other concert halls, nor even for the theatres. Yes, he would go to the Circus. He hadn't been there for ten days.

For years Jules Le Baron had attended the *Cirque Parisien* at least once a fortnight; his friends used to chaff him for his fondness for it. Those who had known him from a boy liked to remind him of his first great ambition—to be a performer on the trapeze. Though this amused him now, he had never lost his love for feats of daring and skill. Whenever he felt particularly tired from his work at the wool-house, he would go to the Circus; it refreshed him, and he fancied that it made him sleep well afterwards. His first love had been a beautiful Roumanian, who jumped through hoops of fire, landing on her velvet-caparisoned horse, without even singeing her long, blond hair. He was fifteen then, and he discovered that the lady was forty-five, though he could have sworn there was not a difference of more than three years in their ages. Since that time he had become enamoured of many of the glittering amazons of the arena, who shot through the air, or through hoops, or out of the mouths of cannons, or crossed dizzy heights on the tight-rope, or juggled with long, villainous-looking knives falling in showers into their hands.

Those episodes, however, brightened Jules Le Baron's life long before he was twenty-five. He had since had many similar experiences in the larger arena of the world. Indeed, he gloried in his susceptibility; he used to give people to understand that, though fairly successful in business, he had a very keen appreciation of the sentiments, and of all the refinements of life. To a foreigner he would have expressed this complication by saying that he was Parisian to his finger-tips. In America, where, at the age of twenty-six, he passed three wretched months, he had been appalled by the lack of sentiment among the people. Of course, as he represented there the wool-house with which he had been connected since his sixteenth year, he met chiefly business men; but even these ought to have displayed an interest in something outside their commercial routine.

It was those three months in America that gave Jules Le Baron his zest for Paris. Of course, he had always loved it; but till he left it, his love had not become self-conscious. America taught him what he had only dimly known before, that for him Paris was the only city in the world worth living in. He knew that people born away from Paris liked other cities; secretly, however, this amused him. He believed that no one, after living in Paris, could find any other place habitable. Indeed, any places, any people, any customs foreign to Paris seemed to him so droll that at the thought of some of them he often laughed aloud. America had given him things to laugh at for the rest of his life.

Of course, Jules was proud of having visited America; it gave him a delightful feeling of superiority to his friends and acquaintances at home.

He always felt pleased when the English and Americans that he met in business complimented him on his English; it enabled him to say carelessly: "Oh, I just picked it up when I was in America." He really had learned very little English there; nearly all he knew had been taught him by his father, a professor of chemistry in a small school in Paris, who had spent six months in England during the siege. He had acquired there, however, a smattering of American slang; on his lips it sounded delicious. His friends in Paris thought he spoke English beautifully, and frequently referred to his talent for languages. He had given them glowing accounts of his adventures in America, and said nothing of his desolate loneliness there; so they looked upon him as a born traveller,—as, altogether, a man of remarkable qualities. But for his English and his travels, they would merely have shrugged their shoulders at the mention of his name, and dismissed him with a *"Bon garçon!"*

Jules Le Baron knew that he was much more than a *bon garçon*. His attitude toward the world expressed this; he always acted as if he felt the world had been made exclusively for him. After losing his father at fourteen, he promptly proceeded to link his mother in the closest bonds of slavery. Yet he was kind to her, too, and, in his way, he loved her, for she was made to obey, just as he had been born to command. When she died and left him alone at the age of twenty with a small property, he took a miniature apartment in the *rue de Lisbonne*, and adjusted himself to his new life. His salary at the wool-house, where his English helped to make him valuable, together with the property, gave him an income of ten thousand francs a year. He considered himself rich, a personage, one who ought to marry well.

Jules had thought so much about marriage that, at thirty, it was surprising he should have remained unwedded. Every young woman he met he regarded as a candidate for his hand, and he spent a large part of his leisure in rejecting these innocent suitors. Even now, as he slowly made his way up the *Boulevard*, he fancied that the girls he passed were looking at him admiringly and enviously. He often smiled back at them, for he was rarely unkind and he never gratuitously wounded any one's feelings. With his mother, it is true, he had been occasionally severe, but merely to discipline her, to make her see things as he saw them. At this moment he felt particularly amiable. He was in Paris, on the *Boulevard* that he loved, surrounded by the people that he loved, in the atmosphere which, as he had discovered in America, was as the very breath to his being. The spectacle was all for him! Paris, had been created that he might enjoy it!

Chapter II

Saturday was the fashionable night at the *Cirque Parisien*, and the night when Jules usually attended it. This was Tuesday, however, and Jules decided not to be fashionable, but simply to amuse himself. As he approached the letters of light that flashed the name of the *Cirque* into the eyes of the *boulevardiers*, he suddenly remembered that he had promised to meet two of his comrades of the wool-house in the evening. He turned into the *rue Taitbout*, and as he was walking slowly through the long passageway leading into one of the large apartment-houses there, he felt himself suddenly seized in the darkness by two pairs of hands. He looked quickly around, and dimly recognized Dufresne and Leroux, who had come up from behind him. They were both types, short and swarthy, with oily faces, thick black moustaches, and pointed beards.

"Why didn't you come before?" and "We've been waiting an hour," they cried together.

"He's been up to some adventure, I'll wager," said Leroux.

"Answer! The truth! No lies!" Dufresne exclaimed, shaking him by one shoulder.

Jules pulled away with an effort.

"I thought you were going to rob me!" he laughed.

"You see, he doesn't answer," said Dufresne. "I told you he was up to some adventure."

"Up to some adventure!" Jules repeated. "I've just been taking dinner, and I forgot I'd promised to meet you to-night. Where are you going?"

"We're going to the *Folies Bergères*, and then to a masked ball in Montmartre," Leroux answered, resuming his grip. "Come along."

Jules pulled away with a laugh.

"Thanks. Not to-night. I don't feel like it. Besides, I'm not dressed."

"But *we're* not dressed," they cried together, throwing open their coats. "You won't have to dress. Come on."

Jules shook his head decidedly.

"No," he insisted, "it's all very well for you young bucks. I'm too old. It tires me out for the next day; can't do my work. I think I'll look in at the Circus. Come along with me."

They scoffed at the idea of going to the Circus, and tried to persuade him to accompany them, since he had kept them waiting so long. But he resisted, and, as he turned away from them, they clutched at him again, but he escaped, laughing, into the street, and he saw them shaking their fists after him. Those two "boys," as he called them, were always trying to drag him into their escapades. They looked so much alike that at the office they were called "the twins," and they were always getting into scrapes and into debt together.

Before buying his ticket for the Circus, Jules looked carefully over the program on the posters in the long entrance. Some of the performers he had already seen and the names of a few of them were unfamiliar to him. One name was printed in larger letters than the others—Mademoiselle Blanche. Jules read the paragraph printed below, announcing Mademoiselle Blanche as the most marvellous acrobat in the world, and proclaiming that, in addition to giving her act on the trapeze, she would plunge backward from the top of the theatre, a height of more than seventy-five feet, into a net below. Jules smiled, and felt a thrill of his old boyish excitement at the prospect of seeing the feat performed.

When he turned to buy his ticket, he noticed a large photograph on an easel, standing near the box-office. The name of Mademoiselle Blanche, printed under it, attracted him. The acrobat, her long sinuous limbs encased in white tights, was suspended in mid-air, one arm bent at the elbow, clinging to a trapeze. The tense muscles of the arm made a curious contrast with the expression of the face, which was marked by unusual simplicity and gentleness. The profile was clear, the curving eyelashes were delicately outlined, and the eyes were large and dark. Something about the lines of the small mouth attracted Jules. He studied the picture carefully to discover what it was. The whole expression of the face seemed to him to be concentrated in the mouth; he felt sure that the teeth were small and very white, and the woman's voice was soft and musical. The face differed from the ordinary types of performers he had seen; it reminded him of the faces of some of the girls in the convent of Beauvais, where his mother had once taken him to visit his cousin. The woman must be clever to make herself up so attractively. He wondered if the appearance of youth that she presented was also due to her cleverness. She might easily pass for twenty. Her figure looked marvellously supple; she had probably been trained for the circus from infancy, and she might be fifty years old.

He decided not to buy a seat, but to go into the balcony where he could walk about and look down at the performance. If it bored him, he could rest on one of the velvet-cushioned seats till a new "turn" began. He found more people in the balcony than he had ever seen there before; as a rule they made only a thin fringe around the railing; now they were five and six deep. He established himself beside a post where he could catch glimpses of the arena and get a support, and there he remained for half an hour.

To-night, however, the antics of the clown, the phenomenal intelligence of the performing dogs, even the agility of the Schaeffer family of acrobats, did not interest him. He was impatient to see Mademoiselle Blanche. Her name stood last on the program; she was probably reserved for a crowning attraction. Jules dropped on one of the velvet cushions, and rested there for another half-hour. Then some knife-throwing attracted him, and he slowly worked his way through the crowd to a place where he could look down at the performers. The knife-throwing was followed by an exhibition of trick-riding, which preceded the acrobat's appearance.

Before this appearance took place, however, there was a long wait caused by the preparations made for the great plunge. A thick rope was suspended from one of the beams that supported the roof of the building, and under it a net was spread. Then the half-dozen trapezes that had been tied to the walls, were loosened, and as they swung in the air and the band played, Mademoiselle Blanche, in white silk tights, with two long strips of white satin ribbon dangling from her throat, ran into the ring, and bowed in response to the applause of the crowd.

Jules Le Baron drew a long breath. The long supple limbs, the firm white arms and throat, the pale oval face, framed in dark hair that curled around the forehead, created a kind of beauty that seemed almost ethereal. The glamour of youth was over her, too; she could not be, at most, more than twenty. As she ran up the little rope ladder to the net and climbed hand over hand along the rope to one of the trapezes, Jules thought he had never seen such grace, such exquisite sureness of movement and agility. After reaching the trapeze, she sat there for a moment, smiling and rubbing her hands. Then she began to swing gently, and a moment later she shot through the air to another trapeze several feet away, and from that she passed on to the others with a bewildering swiftness.

Jules had never seen a woman perform alone on the trapeze before, and this exhibition of skill and resource fascinated him. The feats were nearly all new, and some of them of unusual difficulty. When the girl had finished her performance on the trapeze she returned to the rope, and began to pose on it, twisting it around her waist, and hanging suspended with her arms in the air. In this way she rolled gently down to the net.

The event of the evening was yet to come, however. After resting for a moment, Mademoiselle Blanche seized the rope again, and, hand over hand, she climbed to the top of the building; there she sat on a beam, so far from the audience that she seemed much smaller than she really was. The ring-master, a greasy-looking Frenchman in evening dress, appeared in the arena and commanded silence.

"Mademoiselle Blanche must have perfect quiet," he cried, "in order to perform her great feat. The least noise might disturb her, and cause her death."

Jules smiled at this speech; it was very clever, he thought. Of course, it was made merely to impress the audience. He wondered how Mademoiselle Blanche felt at that moment, perched up there so quietly, ready to hurl herself into the air. He did not have time to think much about this, for as he strained his eyes toward her, the signal for the fall was given, the white figure plunged backward, spun to earth, landed with a tremendous thump in the padded net, bounded into the air again, and Mademoiselle Blanche was bowing and kissing her fingers.

For a moment not a sound was heard. Then the audience burst into applause, and Jules Le Baron breathed. He felt as if his heart had stopped beating. He had never seen such a thrilling exhibition before. All his old delight in the circus had come back to him. As he walked out with the crowd, he congratulated himself on not having gone with Dufresne and Leroux. He would not have missed his evening for a dozen balls in Montmartre!

At the door he met Roger Durand, dramatic critic of the *Jour*. He had known Durand as a boy, and they had continued on a footing of half-hostile friendship.

"So you've come to see the new sensation?" said the journalist, as they shook hands.

"Just by chance," Jules replied. "I've never been more surprised in my life. Who is she?"

"That's just what I haven't been able to find out. I've been talking about her tonight with old Réju—he's the man who makes the engagements—but he didn't seem to know much more about her than I did. He said he first heard of her in Bucharest. She made a hit there, too, some time last year."

"But she's French, isn't she? Parisian?"

"She's French, but Réju says she isn't Parisian—comes from the provinces somewhere. There's a woman goes about with her, her mother, I suppose. Réju says mamma keeps her down here," the journalist added with a smile, making a significant gesture with his thumb. "Mamma gets all the money, and Mademoiselle does all the work."

Jules shrugged his shoulders. "Going to your office?" he said. "You have to turn night into day, haven't you?"

"My dear fellow, night is the best part of life. Days were made for sleep. We've got mixed up, that's all, and only a few of us are clever enough to find it out. Come and have a glass of absinthe with me before I go back."

Jules shook his head.

"Some other time. A glass of absinthe would spoil me for to-morrow. *Au revoir.*"

He was glad to be alone again so that he might think over the evening. The beautiful figure whirling through the air still haunted him. "Mademoiselle Blanche!" The name seemed to sing in his mind. He wondered what her real name was. So she had a mother who kept her under her thumb! Then he wondered what she was like out of the circus—ignorant and vulgar, probably, like the rest of them. Yet in her looks she was certainly different from the rest. At any rate, he must go and see her performance again. He would go several times.

Chapter III

When Jules arrived home he found supper on the table of his little dining-room. Madeleine, the old woman who had served his mother for years and remained with him after his mother's death, always left something for him at night. Now he turned away from it in disgust. His face was burning; he felt nervous, excited. After going to bed, he was unable to sleep. He kept seeing Mademoiselle Blanche tumbling through the air! He could not think of her except as in motion. He tried to recall her as she stood in the net, just before climbing the rope to the trapeze, but her figure was vague and shadowy. Then he tried to think out her features as he had observed them, and he found that he had quite forgotten her face; all that remained was an impression of sweetness, of a ravishing smile.

When, finally, he fell asleep, he dreamed of her, still flashing through the air, striking with a thud the padded net, and bouncing to her feet again. He woke several times and felt impatient with himself for not being able to drive the thought away; yet when he sank again into sleep, the dream came back persistently.

At half-past seven he rose, tired from his broken rest. He went at once to the long mirror that covered the door of his wardrobe, expecting to be confronted with the face of an invalid. His gray eyes were slightly inflamed and his cheeks had more than their usual color; otherwise his appearance was normal. For several moments he surveyed himself. As a rule he did not think much about his looks; he knew that he was considered handsome, and this gave him a half-unconscious gratification. When he wanted to please a woman he seldom failed. Now he had a distinct pleasure at the sight of the aristocratic curve of his nose, the strong outline of his chin, the full red lips under his thick brown moustache. Jules wished that he could keep from growing fat; but after all, he reflected philosophically, there was a difference in fatness; some men it made gross and vulgar; his own complexion, however, was so fair that he could never look gross. Even now there was a suggestion about him of the sleekness of a well-kept pigeon.

When he went out to breakfast he found Madeleine looking doleful. Madeleine had known Jules from birth and considered herself a second mother to him. She was short and stout, with a mouthful of very bad teeth, some of which rattled when she spoke, as if they were about to fall out.

"Monsieur Jules did not eat last night," she said as she poured his coffee and pushed his rolls into the centre of the little table.

"No, Madeleine, I wasn't hungry." Jules took up the *Figaro* that was lying on the table and began to look for a reference to Mademoiselle Blanche.

"The coffee will grow cold, Monsieur Jules."

Jules did not hear her. When preoccupied, he had a habit of ignoring Madeleine. Yet, in his way, he liked her; he often wondered what he would do without her; she was docile and attentive to his wants as his mother had been, and she was very inexpensive. For five minutes he read; then, when he found no reference to the acrobat, he threw down the paper with an exclamation of impatience, and seized his cup and sipped his coffee.

"It's cold!" he cried.

Madeleine's look of distress deepened.

"Let me take that away," she said. "I'll get another cup."

When she brought the cup and poured some of the hot coffee into it, Jules drained it, and pushed his chair away from the table.

"But you have eaten nothing, Monsieur Jules!"

"I'm not hungry this morning."

"And you didn't eat anything last night," the old woman repeated, following him with her eyes. "Are you sick?"

"No, no!" Jules replied, impatiently. "I don't feel like eating, that's all. Give me my hat and coat, Madeleine; I shall be late if I don't hurry."

"Monsieur Jules doesn't look well," said Madeleine timidly, as she helped him on with his coat.

"Oh, don't worry about me." At the door Jules turned. "I shall be out late again to-night, Madeleine. You needn't leave the light burning."

The wool-house of Ballou, Mercier & Co., where Jules worked, was only ten minutes' walk from the *rue de Lisbonne*. On his way there, Jules resolved to say nothing to the twins about Mademoiselle Blanche. Of course, Leroux would ask him about the evening, and he would say simply that he had been rather bored. He wanted to keep Mademoiselle Blanche to himself. He even hoped that her performance would not be noised abroad, that she would not become one of those women whom all Paris went to see and every one talked glibly about. But she must be well-known already; it was evidently her performance that had crowded the Circus.

At the office the twins had a great deal to say about the masked ball of the previous night, but Jules hardly heard them. He was still so haunted by the thought of Mademoiselle Blanche that he made several mistakes in his letters; since his return from America he had been placed in charge of all the English correspondence, and it was important that he should be exact. The day had never seemed so long to him, nor his work, in which he usually took pride, so dull. He was impatient for the evening. When six o'clock came, he hurried away without bidding the twins good-night.

Jules walked toward the little restaurant in the *Boulevard* where he had dined the night before. He wanted to see André again, to talk over Mademoiselle Blanche with him. He felt almost a personal affection for André now. The little *garçon* was bewildered by Jules' affability, and overcome by the generous tip which he received as Jules left the place. Indeed, freed from the labors of the day, Jules felt buoyant and happy. But when he reached the Circus, his spirits sank; he had forgotten that Mademoiselle Blanche did not appear till nearly eleven. He would have to wait for her at least three hours!

He felt so vexed that he turned away from the theatre and walked along the *Boulevard*. It was late in October, and a light rain was falling, mixed with snow. The *Boulevard* was crowded with people, hurrying under umbrellas. Jules turned up the collar of his overcoat, and shivered. What was he to do till eleven? He might go to one of the theatres, but he would not enjoy it. When he reached the *Opéra*, he had not made up his mind what to do, and he walked on as far as the Madeleine. He entered a *café* opposite the church, and called for a bock and one of the illustrated papers. For an hour he sat there, sipping the beer and pretending to read. The jokes, however, which he usually enjoyed, seemed to him vulgar. He was thinking of the figure in white silk tights, shooting through the air. A score of times he called himself a fool for not being able to put that thought out of his mind; yet he felt nervous and irritable, simply because he was impatient to see the spectacle again. At last he became so uneasy that he looked for the waiter to pay his bill and leave. Then he felt a slap on the shoulder, and Durand's smiling face confronted him.

There was no reason why Jules should have been displeased at seeing Durand; yet at that moment he felt resentful. The journalist was small and dapper, with the ends of his black moustache carefully waxed. His little black eyes were always sparkling with humor, and when he smiled he showed two rows of regular white teeth. Yet, in spite of the care of himself which he seemed to take, he never looked quite clean; his thick black hair was always dusty with dandruff, which fell on the shoulders of his coat. He spoke in a high thin voice and with a patronizing air that exasperated Jules.

"I thought I recognized your back," he said, when Jules had turned his face toward him.

Jules grunted and pointed to a chair at the little table. He wanted to show by his manner that he didn't like that familiar slap. Durand, however, was unruffled.

"What are you doing here, anyway? Why aren't you at the theatre or one of the *cafés chantants*?"

Jules took a puff of his cigarette, and then looked down at the little figure.

"I might ask you the same question."

"Oh, I'm working. This is a busy night for me." Then Durand's face lighted. "What do you suppose I've got to do to-night?"

Jules knocked the ashes of his cigarette against the edge of the table. "Now, do you mean? I can't imagine. You're always doing impossible things."

"I'm going to interview the little acrobat."

Jules came very near jumping. He controlled himself, however, and carelessly lifted the cigarette to his lips again.

"What little acrobat?" he asked, screwing his eyes.

"The one you saw last night—at the *Cirque*—the *Cirque Parisien*."

"Oh, Mademoiselle—Mademoiselle—what's her name—the one who dives from the top of the building?"

"Yes, Mademoiselle Blanche. When I went back to the office last night, I told old Bargy about her—cracked her up to the skies, and he swallowed the bait, and sent me round to interview her to-night. Ah, my dear boy, that's one of the advantages of being a newspaper man. It opens every door to you. Whenever I want to get acquainted with a pretty actress, I simply go and interview her."

He sat back in his seat and smiled and hummed a popular song, rapping the table with his fingers. The waiter came up and asked for his order.

"Two bocks!" said Durand, looking at Jules.

"No, no more for me. I haven't finished this yet." When the waiter went away, Jules glanced sleepily at the journalist. "You're a very lucky fellow, it seems to me. I should think it would be rather agreeable to know the pretty actresses."

Durand shrugged his shoulders. "Sometimes, yes—sometimes, no. Usually it spoils the illusion."

Jules stared thoughtfully at his bock. "Aren't you afraid you'll be disillusioned by Mademoiselle Blanche?"

"Oh, probably. They're all alike—when you come to know them. But there's something about her that made me think she might be a little different from the rest. At any rate, she's dev'lish pretty, isn't she?"

"Do you think so?" Jules asked, with a deprecating lift of the eyebrows.

"Think so! I know so! If you don't think so you must be hard to please."

"Oh, I thought she was pretty in her circus rig. I should like to see her out of the ring. They make up so, those women. You can't tell whether they're really pretty or not."

"Well, come around with me, and I'll introduce you. Then you can see for yourself."

Jules nearly jumped again, but his cigarette helped him to disguise the impulse. "I'm afraid I shall be in the way," he said, after a meditative puff.

Durand had seized the bock left on the table by the waiter, and was holding it over his head. When half the contents had disappeared, he smacked his lips and wiped them with his handkerchief. "Not at all. You'll help me draw her out. They say she does the shy-young-girl act; so she's hard to talk with. That seems to be a favorite pose of actresses nowadays."

Jules' heart was throbbing. He was afraid that Durand would discover his elation. So he tried to appear indifferent and cynical. Durand's cynicism amused him; yet in the journalist's presence he was always trying to imitate it.

When he had drained his bock, Durand stood up, surveyed with a professional eye the crowd at the tables, nodded to a few acquaintances, and made a sign to Jules that he was ready to go. It had ceased raining, but the sky was still leaden. The splendid portico of the Madeleine loomed out of the darkness, and the lights in the *Boulevard des Capucines* were gleaming faintly in the mist. They met few people as they walked toward the *Opéra*, but there was plenty of life around the theatres in the *Boulevard des Italiens*. When they reached the *Cirque*, Durand had a whispered consultation with the *Control* who sat in self-conscious dignity and evening dress at the desk near the main door. He referred the journalist to a short fat man with a white beard, lounging a few feet away, and Jules stood apart while the two had an animated talk. After a few moments, Durand made a sign to Jules to come up, and Jules found himself presented to Réju as "my *confrère*, Monsieur Jules Le Baron, of the Marseilles *Gazette*." Réju was very amiable, and Jules felt angry, though he could not help being amused by Durand's serene impudence.

They were conducted at once into the theatre, under the great arch, draped with French flags, where the performers made their exits and their entrances. Then they found themselves in a large bare room, with several passages radiating from it.

"The dressing-rooms are here," Réju explained, pointing to the passages. "Mademoiselle Blanche's room is number 5. I don't know whether she has come yet or not. Her act doesn't begin till ten minutes of eleven. Wait here, and I'll see if she can receive you."

Durand smiled at Jules, and as soon as Réju was out of hearing, he whispered: "I hope you didn't mind that little fairy-tale of mine. I had to pass you off as one of the fraternity. If I hadn't they wouldn't have let you come in. Now, don't forget your part, the Marseilles *Gazette*. It's a good republican paper. The editor's a great friend of mine."

"I'm afraid I sha'n't be a credit to the profession. I've never seen any one interviewed in my life."

"Then it'll be an education to you." Durand laughed. "Look out. Here he comes!"

The fat little manager approached them with a smiling face; he evidently had in mind two free advertisements for the theatre.

"Mademoiselle Blanche," he said impressively, "arrived five minutes ago, and she hasn't begun to dress yet. If you'll have the kindness to follow me, messieurs"—he concluded with a bow and a wave of the hand.

Jules' body was tingling, and his heart beat violently. Durand, on the contrary, seemed more debonair than ever; with an air of importance, he strutted behind the manager, as if conferring an honor on the performer by his call. Réju rapped on the door, and after a moment a shrill voice piped:

"Entrez!"

Chapter IV

Durand made a bold entrance, and Jules followed sheepishly. The room was small and uncarpeted; on one side stood a wardrobe and a table, and on the opposite wall hung a large mirror that reflected nearly the whole of the apartment. The rest of the furniture consisted of two wooden chairs and a large trunk. Jules did not realize that he had observed these details till afterward, for his glance was bent on the face of Mademoiselle Blanche, who stood beside the trunk, surveying her callers with apprehension in her big eyes. On one of the chairs sat a woman of fifty, tall and thin, with strands of flesh hanging at her neck, her eyes bright, her lips aglow with a false bloom, and her cheeks pallid with powder. Jules recognized her at once as the acrobat's mother, and he had a shock of surprise and revulsion.

The manager, after presenting the callers to Madame Perrault, and then to her daughter, excused himself with a flourish, and left the room. Madame Perrault was smiling and chattering at Durand, and Mademoiselle Blanche was flushed and confused.

"I think we must be the first of the Parisian journalists to interview Mademoiselle," said Durand to the mother, letting his eyes turn vaguely to the acrobat for information.

Madame Perrault gave a little jump, and glanced hastily at her daughter's face.

"Yes, you are," she replied. "We did have—that is, there was a gentleman of the press who wanted to interview Blanche, but she—she was a little timid about it. Blanche is very timid; so we—we put it off. But interviewers are very— —Ah, you will sit down, will you not?" she said to Jules, who had remained standing with his eyes fixed on the girl.

Mademoiselle Blanche had taken a seat on the trunk, and her mother sat beside her so that Jules might occupy her chair. When they were all adjusted, Madame Perrault resumed, turning to Jules, whose embarrassment she had observed.

"Monsieur Réju told me yesterday interviews were so important. They make people interested. They— —"

"But the people are already interested in Mademoiselle Blanche," Durand interposed, gallantly. "That's why my *confrère* and I have come here.

The Parisians want to know all about Mademoiselle. She's the sensation of the hour. Her name is on everybody's lips."

He glanced at Mademoiselle Blanche with his most languishing smile, and Jules felt a sudden desire to kick him. The acrobat tried to look pleased, but she succeeded only in appearing more confused. Jules was surprised to see how frail she was. Her figure, full and vigorous in the ring, seemed so thin in her plain, tight-fitting gray dress, that he felt sure she must have been padded for her performance.

"I'm going to ask Mademoiselle a great many questions," Durand resumed, still leering at the acrobat.

"But I have nothing to tell," she replied, speaking for the first time.

"But you must have been born, and grown up, and done a great many things besides, that the rest of us don't do," the journalist laughed, growing more familiar. Jules' dislike for him was rapidly developing into hatred.

Durand's familiarity, however, seemed to please the acrobat's mother.

"Blanche is too modest," she said. "She's had a great many things happen to her."

"Have you always been in the circus, Mademoiselle?"

"Yes, ever since she was a child," her mother answered. "Her father was an acrobat."

"So it's in the family. And were you in the circus too, Madame?"

Madame Perrault shook her head, and Jules thought he saw her blush under the powder. "No, I have never been in public life. My husband's family lived in Boulogne, where I lived too. They were all acrobats. After my marriage I used to travel with the circus, and when Blanche was born, Monsieur Perrault wanted her to perform, too. When she was only five years old, they used to appear together."

"Then you have travelled a great deal, Mademoiselle?" Durand turned his fascinating glance on the girl. She looked at her mother, and as she was about to reply, Madame Perrault resumed: "Ah, my daughter has been over nearly the whole world,—in England, in Germany, in Russia—"

"Have you ever been in America?" Jules asked quickly.

The acrobat shook her head.

"But she has had such offers—such splendid—such magnificent offers to go there," the mother cried, clasping her hands.

"But I'm afraid," the girl murmured, glancing at Jules with her big timid eyes.

"Afraid of the voyage?" Jules asked. Her eyes were still fixed upon him, and he felt as if every nerve in his body were vibrating. "That's nothing. I have made it twice, and I wasn't sick a day."

This was not true, for on each trip Jules had been sick for several days; but he made the remark with such ease, that for the moment he felt convinced himself of its truth. Mademoiselle Blanche looked at him admiringly, and he saw that he had made an impression on the mother, too, established himself in her regard as a travelled person, a man of importance.

"Then Monsieur has been in America?" said Madame Perrault.

"Oh, yes," Jules replied, carelessly. "All over it. It's a wonderful country."

Mademoiselle Blanche sighed, and her mother glanced at her wistfully.

"But it's too far," Madame resumed with a shake of the head. "We could not go so far from the children."

"Then you have other children?" said the journalist. "Are they in the circus, too?"

For the first time, the girl's face brightened. "Oh, no!" she replied, with a suggestion of horror in her tone.

"They are very young," the mother explained. "Jeanne is only fourteen and Louise will be eleven next month. They are with my sister in Boulogne."

Durand made a little sign of impatience which indicated to Jules that he was not getting the information he wanted. Besides, he was evidently displeased by the failure of his leers to produce any apparent effect upon the girl; she seemed to be unconscious of them.

"And Monsieur Perrault," he said, "he is still performing?"

An expression of pain appeared in the mother's face, and Mademoiselle dropped her eyes.

"No, he died three years ago," Madame Perrault replied. "He was killed at Monte Carlo. He fell from the trapeze."

There was silence for a moment, and the journalist tried to infuse into his insipid little face a look of sympathy. Just how much sympathy he felt was shown by his next remark.

"I couldn't help wondering last night," he said briskly, "when I saw Mademoiselle perform, how she felt just before she took that plunge. How do you feel, Mademoiselle? Aren't you frightened, just a little?"

The girl shook her head. "I have done it for so many years, I don't think of being afraid. My father taught me never to have the least fear. He wouldn't have been killed if the trapeze hadn't broken."

"And we take every precaution," Madame Perrault quickly explained.

Durand began to ask questions about the various cities Mademoiselle had visited. Most of the replies came from Madame Perrault, who seemed to have constituted herself her daughter's mouthpiece. Which audiences did she like best to play to? The Germans! Durand shook his head. He wouldn't dare to say that in a French paper. It might make Mademoiselle unpopular with the Parisians. Ah, but Mademoiselle liked the Parisians, too. Didn't she find them very enthusiastic? No? That was simply because they were thrilled, overcome, silenced by her performance. Durand grew excited in extolling the merits of Parisian audiences. For their favorites they would do anything, and Mademoiselle was fast becoming one of the most popular of their favorites. Of course they had their peculiarities. When a performer vexed them, there were no limits to their wrath. Had Mademoiselle heard of the attack on Sophie Lenoir at the *Ambassadeurs*? The audience had thrown at her everything they could lay hands on, and she had fainted, or pretended to faint, on the stage.

Indeed, much of the conversation was supplied by the journalist himself. He had apparently abandoned hope of making the acrobat talk; so he addressed most of his speeches to the mother, whom he drew out by many artful devices. Mademoiselle Blanche sat looking on in open-eyed surprise, as if she did not have a share in the matters under discussion. Occasionally she would glance appealingly at Jules; when he looked back, she would blush and turn her head away.

While Durand was in the middle of one of his stories, Madame Perrault drew a small gold watch from her pocket. The journalist jumped from his chair.

"We are keeping Mademoiselle from dressing," he said, as Jules rose, too. "A thousand pardons. We will go in just a moment. There's only one more question. That is about your presents, Mademoiselle, your gifts."

"My gifts?" the acrobat repeated vaguely.

"Yes, from the princes, the crowned heads you've appeared before."

"Ah!" the mother exclaimed, in a long breath, "Blanche has received so many! There was the brooch from the Emperor of Russia, and the ring from the Prince of Roumania, a costly diamond, monsieur, so clear and beautiful, and the little gold watch studded with pearls from the King of Bavaria, the 'mad King' they call him, you know—and then—then the bracelet set with rubies from the Duchess of Merlino, when Blanche was in Bucharest. Ah, but we have none of these here. They are all at home, they—"

"Here in Paris?" Durand asked, impatiently.

"No, monsieur, in Boulogne," Madame Perrault answered, and Jules saw an expression of wonder and pain cross her daughter's face.

Durand was rubbing his silk hat with his glove, and regarding it intently.

"Then," he said, looking up quickly, "there must have been some adventures—some admirers, that have followed Mademoiselle, perhaps, eh?" he added, leering insinuatingly at the mother.

Madame smiled, and the face of the acrobat turned pink. Jules wanted to seize the little journalist by the neck, and throw him out of the door.

"Ah, in Bucharest," cried Madame, "the young—"

"Mamma!"

Madame Perrault shrugged her shoulders, and smiled suggestively. "Perhaps we'd better not speak of that. Blanche is a good girl," she added, patting her daughter on the back. "She's good to her mother, and she's good to her sisters. Ah, *ma chère*!"

The girl had turned her head away. Durand offered her his hand gallantly, and then beamed on the mother. "I will come and see you some time, if you will give me permission," he said condescendingly.

"Some Sunday," Madame Perrault replied. "It's the only day when Blanche is free. And you will bring your friend, perhaps, if he is still in Paris," she added amiably, with a quick glance and smile at the journalist from Marseilles. Then she produced two cards and passed them to the callers.

Jules murmured a civil response to the invitation, and, after bowing low to the ladies, he followed Durand and closed the door behind him. The expression of languishing pleasure in the journalist's face had given place to a look of hilarious merriment.

"Did you ever see such a block? She didn't have a word to say. I don't believe she has an idea. And she thought she was impressing me with her modesty! And the gifts from the crowned heads—wasn't that droll? Of course, the old lady made up every one of those stories. She's a sharp one, with her painted lips and her powdered cheeks. Her little game is to get a rich husband for the girl, and I'll wager a week's salary she'll succeed."

Jules said nothing. He knew it would be useless to argue with Durand. If he were to give his opinion of Mademoiselle Blanche, the journalist would laugh, and say he didn't understand women, especially actresses. So, when Durand suddenly asked him what he thought of the girl, he merely shrugged his shoulders.

As they passed out they met Réju, who offered them seats if they cared to remain for the rest of the performance. Durand explained that he must return at once to the office, and urged Jules to accept the invitation. When Jules found himself alone in the first row of the orchestra he breathed with relief. He had never before realized what an odious little creature Durand was. For the moment he forgot even to feel gratitude for the introduction to the acrobat.

He was unable to take an interest in the performance, and he looked at his watch to see how long he would have to wait for the appearance of Mademoiselle Blanche. It was just twenty minutes past ten. Suddenly it occurred to him that he would have time to go out and buy some flowers for her. He left his seat, and hurried to the nearest shop in the *Boulevard*. There he bought the finest bunch of white roses he could find, went back to the theatre, and sent them to the acrobat with his card. When at last Mademoiselle Blanche ran into the arena, he was thrilled with joy. She wore his flowers in her belt.

Chapter V

That night Jules Le Baron knew that for the first time in his life he was really in love. He had often fancied himself in love before, and he had enjoyed the experience; now he discovered his mistake. Love was not the pure delight he had imagined it to be. It is true, he had moments of ecstasy, of sublime self-congratulation, when he felt with stronger conviction that the world was made for him and he had been created to conquer the world; but during the next few days these were followed by long periods of depression, of abject despair.

At times, too, the grotesqueness of this infatuation appalled him. To be in love with an acrobat, a woman who earned her bread by hurling herself from the top of a building, who risked her life every day, sometimes twice a day, that she might live! Then, at the thought of her amazing courage, Jules would be overcome, and if alone in his room at home, he would throw himself on the bed, bury his head in the pillow and groan. Indeed, at this period he went through many strange and violent performances. Madeleine became alarmed for his health, and thought of sending for a doctor.

He could not apply himself to his work; he made so many mistakes in his English correspondence that Monsieur Mercier had to ask him to be more careful. The twins noticed his condition and chaffed him, and insisted on knowing "her name"; in secret they decided that Jules had been investing his money badly; he had often boasted to them about his little property. They tried to cheer him by urging him to join them in their nocturnal expeditions, but he always replied that he was staying at home in the evening now. As a matter of fact, he spent every night or a portion of every night at the *Cirque Parisien*, and at each appearance of Mademoiselle Blanche, he was gratified to see that she wore his nightly offering of roses in her belt. He never received an acknowledgment of these tributes, for he did not dare write his address on the cards he sent with them. Once, as she stood in the net, just before climbing the rope to make her great plunge, he fancied that his eye caught hers, and she smiled at him. He decided afterward that he had been mistaken; but the thought of that smile prevented him from sleeping half the night.

Jules was keeping his courage alive in the hope of seeing her at her apartment on Sunday. His only fear was that Durand would be there.

Durand's published interview with Mademoiselle Blanche was so flippant that it deepened the hatred Jules had already conceived for the journalist. He resolved on Sunday to explain to Madame Perrault that he was not what Durand had represented him to be and to appear in his own character; he was conceited enough to believe that in his own character he could make quite as good an impression as in any other. Besides, had not Mademoiselle Blanche been impressed by the fact that he had visited America?

On Saturday night he sent his silk hat to be blocked, and his frock-coat to be pressed, and he bought a pair of white gloves. Madeleine found him much more agreeable on Sunday morning than he had been during the week; but, though he seemed to be recovering his spirits, she still felt worried. In the afternoon he presented himself before her for inspection, asked if his coat set well, if she liked the colour of his gloves, what she thought of the violets that he wore. She became enraptured over his appearance, told him that he had never looked so beautiful, and saw him go away with a radiant face. Then, as the door closed behind him, she went into her little chamber and wept. The truth had flashed upon her! Her Jules was in love! Some one else was going to take his mother's place and hers. She felt all the jealousy and misery that his own mother might have felt at the moment, combined with a pathetic consciousness that she had no right to grieve. Jules was everything in the world to her, she said to herself, and she was nothing to him. She was an old broken woman, and for the rest of her days she should have to live alone.

Jules had become her pride and the source of her happiness. Yet she really saw very little of him—the only meal he took at home was his breakfast—but she really existed for the pleasure of serving him and looking at his face in the morning. Now, in spite of her misery, she knelt before the statue of the Blessed Virgin that stood on a little table beside her bed, and prayed that the woman who was going to take her place might be a good woman, and worthy of her boy. In her simple affection for Jules she believed that he had only to show that he cared for a woman to have her throw herself into his arms.

It was hardly three o'clock, too early for a call, Jules thought, as he walked toward the *rue St. Honoré*; but he was so impatient to see Mademoiselle Blanche again that he could not wait till later in the afternoon. During the week the sun had hardly appeared, and the succession of leaden skies had helped to depress his spirits. To-day, however, the sky was blue and the sun shone so brightly that it seemed almost like spring. He was in one of his buoyant moods, when he felt sure of his ability to conquer. In his fine clothes and with his confident manner, he looked very handsome; several pretty girls gratified him by staring at him as he passed. If he impressed people he didn't know, why couldn't he impress Mademoiselle Blanche? He planned a great many things to say to her. He would be particularly amiable to the mother, too, and tell her all about America.

The number in the *rue St. Honoré* that Madame Perrault had given corresponded with one of the great white stucco apartment houses abounding in Paris. He passed under the wide vaulted entrance, and asked the wife of the *concierge* if Madame Perrault lived there. "*Au sixième*," was the shrill reply, and he started up the narrow stairs. When he reached the *sixième*, the top floor of the house, he panted and waited for a moment before ringing, to catch his breath. Then he carefully arranged his cuffs, touched with his gloved hand his silk cravat and his flowers and, with a sigh of anticipation, he rang the bell.

A trim little servant of not more than fifteen opened the door. When Jules asked for Madame Perrault, she shook her head.

"She went out an hour ago, monsieur, and she won't be back till four."

Jules' heart sank. Of course, mother and daughter were out together. He was about to turn away despairingly, but he suddenly thought of inquiring if Mademoiselle were at home. The maid nodded.

"Shall I say that monsieur wishes to see her?" she asked, stepping back that he might enter.

"If you please," he replied, as he followed the girl into the little *salon*. It was furnished wholly in Japanese fashion; the walls were hung with Japanese draperies, and a large thick rug covered the floor. On the mantel, prettily draped with a wide piece of flowered silk, stood a number of photographs, one of them a duplicate of the portrait of Mademoiselle Blanche that he had seen in the entrance of the Circus. As Jules glanced at this, he heard a light step in the adjoining room, and when he turned, Mademoiselle Blanche herself was looking at him out of her dark eyes. She walked toward him, flushing a little, and extended her hand.

"I am sorry mamma is not here," she said. "She went out only a few minutes ago, and she'll be back soon. But we—"

"You didn't expect any one so early. I ought to apologize, but I was impatient to come. Then—I—I hoped to find you alone."

"So you have," she laughed, pointing to a chair near the grate-fire. She wore a dress of dark silk with little white spots in it that became her wonderfully, Jules thought. Around her neck was a piece of muslin, open at the throat, and muslin encircled her wrists. Once again Jules was impressed by the delicacy of her appearance; her skin had an almost transparent whiteness, and there was no colour in her cheeks, save when she flushed, which she did at the least cause.

"How pleasantly you are lodged here," said Jules, looking around the room. The apartment was as small as his own, which he had considered one of the smallest in Paris.

"Yes, we were fortunate to get it. And it seems so odd—it belongs to an actress who's spending the winter in the South of France. We have taken it furnished."

"Then you're to be here all the winter?" said Jules, feasting his eyes on the clear white forehead, the white neck that he could see beneath the muslin. How beautiful she was! His surmise about the teeth had been correct; they were small and white, with little bits of red between them.

"No," she replied, "I've been engaged at the *Cirque* until the first of January. Then I shall go to Vienna, and appear there for several months."

"Ah!" For a moment Jules was silent. "But you will take a rest before you go to Vienna?"

She shook her head.

"No. I should like to go home for Christmas to be with my sisters. But they will come to Paris instead."

"But doesn't it tire you?"

"No. It isn't hard. And I never like to stop. I must keep in practice."

For an instant Jules was touched by a curious sympathy. There certainly was something pathetic, even abnormal, in the thought that this frail woman hurled herself six days in the week from the top of a building. Then he was thrilled again by the marvel of it, by the consciousness that he was sitting opposite the phenomenon, gazing into her eyes, hearing her voice, receiving her smiles. He could think of nothing to say, but he felt quite happy; he would have liked to sit there for hours in mute admiration. Mademoiselle Blanche, however, looked confused; she seemed to be shaping something in her mind.

"It was very kind of you to send the flowers," she said at last. "I would have thanked you before if I had known where you lived. They were very lovely."

His face shone with pleasure at the thought that she had recognized him as the sender, and he leaned toward her. "You needn't thank me," he said. "I felt repaid when I saw them in your belt."

Then he told her how he had gone to the circus every night just to see her; how he admired her performance, her grace and skill on the trapeze, her courage in making the great plunge. As he spoke, her face kept changing colour. She seemed to him like a bashful child, and he marvelled at her ingenuousness, for surely she must be used to praise. Then he recalled what

Durand had said about her affectation of modesty, and he wondered if the journalist could have been right; but when he looked into the girl's clear eyes he saw nothing but beauty and truth.

When he had finished speaking of her performance, he began to talk about himself, his favourite topic with women. He told her about his visit in the United States, and he made fun of the Americans for drinking water instead of wine at table, and for many other customs that had amused him because they were so unlike the ways of Parisians. He also imitated the speech of some of the Americans he had known, and he was surprised to find that she understood what he said. She had learned English from her father, she explained; he had often performed in London, and she had been there with him twice. Then he began to speak with her in English to display his accomplishment, and he felt disappointed on discovering that she could converse quite as fluently, and with a better accent. So he returned to French, and told her about his life in Paris, his dear old Madeleine who kept him so comfortable in his little apartment, his work at the office, and about Dufresne and Leroux. She showed no surprise when he revealed Durand's duplicity; she merely said that she hadn't liked the journalist, and her mother had been vexed by the article. She seemed so interested that he went back to his early days, before the death of his father and mother, described his life at the *lycée*, his love of sport, his passion for the circus, his boyish adventures at Montmartre, his happy days in summer at Compiègne, his mother's goodness and her foolish pride in him. He was so unconscious in his egotism that it was touching to hear him; Mademoiselle Blanche seemed to be unconscious of it, too, for she listened with a serious, absorbed attention. While he was in the midst of an analysis of his own qualities, the little clock on the mantel struck four and Mademoiselle Blanche looked up quickly.

"Mamma will be here very soon now," she said.

Jules felt a sudden irritation. At that moment the coming of Madame Perrault seemed like an intrusion. The reference to it had the effect of stopping his confidences; it was as if she had already appeared in the room. He rose from his seat, and began to examine the photographs on the mantel. Then he took up one of them, a large photograph of a man of more than fifty, with a white pointed beard, a shock of iron-grey hair, and laughing eyes.

"Is this your father, mademoiselle?"

She shook her head.

"That is my mother's *fiancé*."

He turned to her quickly. "Your mother's *fiancé*!"

"Yes. My mother has been engaged a long time. She would have been married a year ago but for me."

"Ah, then you don't like it—you don't want her to marry again?"

"I should not care—that is, I should be glad for Jeanne and Louise. Monsieur Berthier is very rich, and he has been kind to the girls. He has offered to give them a home."

Jules came near laughing. It seemed to him ridiculous that the old powdered woman he had seen in the dressing-room of the Circus should marry again.

"Then how have you prevented the marriage?" he asked.

"Because I must work," she replied simply, "and mamma cannot leave me. If mamma married Monsieur Berthier, she would have to stay in Boulogne."

"Ah!" A light broke on Jules. The mother would not marry until her eldest daughter was married. So, of course, she must be anxious to find a husband for Mademoiselle Blanche. He felt as if Providence were paving the way toward happiness for him. For a moment he did not speak again. Then he said: "But you will marry some day, and then your mother won't have to travel with you."

She flushed, and made a deprecating gesture. "I shall always stay in the circus," she said. "It's my life. I can't think of any other."

Then he gradually drew her out. She surprised him by telling him of the monotony of her life. With most of the other performers she had merely a slight acquaintance; the coarseness of the women and the vulgarity of the men shocked her. Her only companion in her travels was her mother. Yes, it was lonely sometimes not to know other girls of her own age, and it was very hard to be separated from Jeanne and Louise. She worried a great deal about Jeanne, who had shown a fondness for the circus. She thought if her mother married, Jeanne would give up all thought of becoming a performer. Of course, it was different with herself; she had been bred to the circus, but she couldn't bear the thought of Jeanne's being there, too. Jeanne was very pretty and lively; Aunt Sophie was obliged to be strict with her. Louise was so different, so quiet and simple, and religious, almost a *dévote*. As she spoke of her sisters, Mademoiselle Blanche grew very animated. Jules blamed himself for the momentary doubt he had felt about her. If Durand could only hear her now! But Durand doubted every woman.

It was nearly five o'clock when Madame Perrault returned. When she saw Jules, she showed no surprise, but smiled upon him broadly and extended her hand. Mademoiselle Blanche lapsed into silence and, as her mother talked, with a superabundance of gesture and with tireless vivacity, she could feel Jules' eyes fixed upon her. She knew that Jules hardly heard what was being said, and when he rose to take his departure, she made no effort to detain him.

"I should like to come again," he said to the girl.

"Some afternoon, perhaps," Madame Perrault suggested amiably. "Blanche always rests between three and four, but after that she could see you."

"But I am at my office till six."

"Ah, yes!" Madame Perrault exclaimed with a smile. "That wicked journalist! You must tell him we were vexed with his article."

"Then may I come in the evening? Perhaps you'll let me take you to the theatre some night?"

Madame Perrault clapped her hands. "That would be perfect!"

Mademoiselle Blanche said nothing, but it was to her that Jules directed his next remark.

"Perhaps to-morrow night; I will come at eight o'clock."

Madame Perrault displayed her gleaming teeth patched with gold, and her daughter merely bowed and said, "Thank you."

As Jules was putting on his overcoat in the little hall, he heard a voice say:

"Il est très gentil, ce monsieur," but though he listened he could not catch the reply. He was radiantly happy, however. When he reached the street, he felt like running; with an effort he controlled himself, and walked buoyantly home with a smile on his face. He would take Madeleine out to dinner, as he used to take his mother when they celebrated his holidays!

Chapter VI

The next night, promptly at eight o'clock, Jules appeared in the little *salon* in the *rue St. Honoré*, bearing his offering of flowers to Mademoiselle Blanche. Madame Perrault gave him the quiet reception of an old friend, and he felt as if he had long been in the habit of calling at the apartment. Madame Perrault informed him that she had just risen from dinner, and asked him to drink a cup of coffee. Then the three figures sat in the dimly-lighted room and talked; that is, Jules and Madame Perrault talked, for Blanche ventured a remark only when a question was put to her.

A few moments later, Madame Perrault went into the next room where she was occupied with the little maid in making a dress; so Jules was left alone with her daughter. They had very little to say to each other, and Jules was content to sit in silence and rapt adoration. As he looked at her, her name kept singing in his mind: Blanche! He wondered if he should ever dare to address her in this way. How beautiful she was as she sat there, the soft light of the fire falling on her face and hands, and on the folds of her gown! He was glad she was so quiet; he hated women that talked all the time. That was the great fault with Madame Perrault; if she said less, he would like her, in spite of her powder and paint. Since hearing that she was engaged, and wanted to get her daughter married, Jules' feelings toward her had softened.

It was nearly ten o'clock before they left for the theatre. Jules called a cab, and all three squeezed into it with a great deal of laughter on the part of Madame Perrault. As they rattled over the rough pavement, the noise was so great that they could not talk, and Jules gave himself up to contemplating the serious face of Mademoiselle Blanche. The thought that he was riding with her to the scene of her triumphs thrilled him. He felt as if he were having a share in her performance, as if her glory were reflected on him. Ah, if Dufresne and Leroux could see him now! How they would be impressed, and how they would envy him!

Before bidding his friends good-night, he asked if he might not take them home; he would remain till the end of the performance, anyway, he said. Instead of entering the theatre at once, he sauntered along the *Boulevard* toward the *place de la Bastille*. What were the other performers to him? Without Mademoiselle Blanche the *Cirque Parisien* would not be worth visiting. He did not return to the theatre till it was nearly time for her to appear. Réju was standing at the door, and made a sign for him to pass in without paying. Jules accepted the invitation with a twinge of conscience. He wondered what Réju would think if he discovered Durand's imposition.

After the performance, Jules waited at the stage-door for half an hour till Mademoiselle Blanche appeared again. Then he asked her and her mother to take supper with him at one of the restaurants in the *Boulevard*. Madame Perrault consented amiably, and they entered a little *café,* where a half-dozen young men and girls were sitting round a table, playing cards. Jules wanted to order a bottle of champagne; but Mademoiselle Blanche objected; he could scarcely keep from smiling when she said she would much rather have beer. So he called for three bocks and some cheese sandwiches, and over this simple repast they became very gay. Madame Perrault was the liveliest of the three, and she amused Jules by a description of her *fiancé,* who had been in love with her, she said, long before her marriage with Blanche's father. She seemed to think it was very droll that he should want to marry her now; she had told him he would do much better to marry Blanche, or to wait till Jeanne grew up. Under the warmth of her humor, Jules' prejudices against her disappeared, and he found himself growing fond of her. At that moment he longed to confide in her, to tell her all about his infatuation for her daughter, and to ask her advice about the best way of pleasing the girl.

When they had left the *café,* and Jules had taken his friends home and dismissed the cab, he fell again into the depression of the week before. As he walked to the *rue de Lisbonne* in the damp night, he blamed Durand for having introduced him to the Perraults. If he hadn't met Mademoiselle Blanche he might have gone on living comfortably, enjoyed his daily work, his little dinners, his visits to the theatre, his comfortable apartment, with Madeleine to look after his wants. Now he was upset, at sea. He hated the routine of the office; the vulgar stories of Dufresne and Leroux disgusted him; the apartment was cold and lonely; Madeleine was always interfering with him. He resolved not to go to the *Cirque* again; he would try to forget Mademoiselle Blanche and her mother's chatter. But when he went to bed it was of her that he thought, and he dreamed that he saw her again, in her white silk tights, climbing hand over hand to the top of the Circus, tumbling through the air, and bouncing with a thud to her feet on the padded net.

The next morning he felt better, and he called himself a fool for his misery of the night before. As he looked back on the evening, he decided that, of course, if they hadn't liked him, they would not have allowed him to take them to the theatre and back, and to a *café* for supper. He wondered what they would think if he called for them again that night. Perhaps it would be better to wait for two or three days. But at the end of the afternoon he felt so impatient to see Mademoiselle Blanche that he determined to risk seeming intrusive. So he bought another bunch of white roses, and at eight o'clock he reappeared in the apartment. Madame Perrault greeted him just as she had done the night before, without a suggestion of surprise in her manner. This made him feel so bold that he did not apologize, as he had intended to do, but took his place by the fire as if he had a right to be there.

In this way, Jules Le Baron's courtship began. It seemed to him a strange courtship. It taught him a great many things,—among others, how little he knew about women. As he had lived in Paris all of his thirty years, with the exception of his three memorable months in America, he thought he understood women; now he saw his mistake. He had not led a particularly good life, though it was so much better than the lives of most of his acquaintances that he considered himself a man of rather superior character. If he had studied his character more carefully, he would have discovered that his superiority was not a matter of morals, but of taste and temperament. Vice seemed to him vulgar, and it made him uncomfortable; so in its grosser forms he had always avoided it. He had, however, the Parisian's frank, ingenuous, almost innocent fondness for the humorously indecent, and his attitude toward life was wholly French. The mention of virtue made him laugh and shrug his shoulders. Most women, he thought, were naturally the inferiors of men; so the better he understood the character of Mademoiselle Blanche, the more surprised he grew. Indeed, there were times when he felt awed in her presence and ashamed of himself. She seemed to know the world and yet to be untainted by it, to turn away instinctively from its evil phases. If her innocence had been ignorant, he could not have respected it; the knowledge that she had lived in the midst of temptation made her goodness seem almost sublime.

Jules fell into the habit of calling for the Perraults in the evening, and he soon became recognized at the *Cirque* as their escort. Réju, who still showed respect for him as a journalist, admitted him to the theatre every night without charge, and he was also permitted to enter the sacred precincts beyond the stage-door, where, instead of waiting on the sidewalk, he stood in a cold corridor, dimly lighted by sputtering lamps. After the performance, he sometimes took his friends into the little *café* for beer and sandwiches, and occasionally Madame Perrault would prepare a supper at home.

Jules' equilibrium became restored again; he made fewer mistakes at the office and he even deceived the twins, who had come to the conclusion that he must be in love. With Madeleine, in spite of his first confidences, he had little to say about Mademoiselle Blanche, and she did not dare ask him questions. His silence and his improved appetite, together with his renewed amiability, made her hope that he had recovered from his infatuation, and she felt easier in mind.

On the Saturday evening following his first call on Mademoiselle Blanche, while Jules was sitting in the little apartment, he asked the girl if they might not pass Sunday together. "We might drive through the *Bois* into the country," he suggested.

She had been looking into the fire, and she glanced at him hesitatingly. "We always go to mass on Sunday morning," she said.

For a moment Jules appeared confused. "But can't you go to early mass?"

Madame Perrault, who was in the next room, called out: "It's no use trying to persuade her not to go to high mass, monsieur. She'd think something terrible was going to happen to her if she didn't go. Now, I go at eight o'clock; so I have the rest of the day free."

Jules looked at Mademoiselle Blanche and smiled, and she smiled back.

"I like to hear the music," she explained apologetically.

"Oh, she's too religious for *this* world," Madame Perrault laughed. "I believe she'd go to mass every morning of her life if she didn't have to stay up so late at night. She ought to be in a convent instead of a circus."

"In a convent!" Jules exclaimed, in mock alarm.

"Don't you ever go to church?" the girl asked, turning to Jules.

He looked confused again. "I? Well, no. To tell the truth, I haven't been in a church for nearly ten years. Oh, yes I have. I went to a funeral two years ago at the Trinity."

"But weren't you—weren't you brought up to go to church?"

"Brought up to go to church? Oh, yes; my mother went to church every Sunday of her life. I used to go with her after my father died."

A long silence followed. Mademoiselle Blanche turned again to the fire, and Jules had a sensation of extreme unpleasantness. Like many Parisians, he never thought about religion. He had been so affected by the skepticism of his associates that he had no real belief in any doctrine. He saw now for the first time that serious complications might arise from his religious indifference. It was very disagreeable, he thought, to be confronted with it in this way. Indeed, the more he thought about it, the more annoyed he became. He felt that he must justify himself in some way. So at last he spoke up: "I suppose you're shocked because I don't go to church, aren't you, mademoiselle?"

Mademoiselle Blanche looked down at her hands lying folded in her lap.

"I'm sorry."

"Sorry?" he repeated, trying to laugh. "Why are you sorry? I rather like it. I never did enjoy going to church."

"We don't go to church to enjoy it, do we?" she asked gently.

He sank back in his seat, and looked at her. "No, I suppose not." Then, after a moment, he suddenly leaned forward. "We can't all be good like you, mademoiselle. Perhaps if I had known you always, I should go to church. I'd do anything to please you."

"But you ought not to go to please me. You ought to go for your own good."

"So you think it does good, then—going to church?"

"I'm sure of it," she replied, gazing into the fire. "Sometimes,—when I feel unhappy because I haven't seen the girls for so long, and because I must be separated from them so much, or when Aunt Sophie complains about Jeanne, or Jeanne has been unkind to Louise, or disobedient, then, after I've been to church, I feel better."

"Why do you feel better?" he asked, more to keep her talking than because he cared for her answer.

"Because I feel sure," she went on, holding her head down, "I feel sure it will all come out right—if I only have faith. Jeanne is a good girl; she's never disobedient or unkind with me."

"Then you worry about Jeanne?"

"Yes—sometimes."

"But you don't worry so much after you've been at church?"

"No."

"And that is why you like to go to church?"

"That's one reason. But there are others—a great many others."

He felt like laughing at the simplicity of her reasoning, and yet he was touched. He had a sudden desire to take her in his arms and stroke her soft hair and tell her he loved her. Then he heard her mother's step in the next room, and this roused him.

"I should like to go to church with you sometimes," he said. "May I?"

"Take him to-morrow, Blanche," cried Madame Perrault, and at that moment Jules could have kissed her, too. "There's going to be a special service at *St. Philippe de Roule* at ten o'clock. The music will be good."

That was how Jules first happened to go to church with Mademoiselle Blanche. After mass they walked up the *Champs Élysées* and then along the *avenue du Bois de Boulogne*, in the midst of the multitude of promenaders. A few of the men recognized the girl, and turned to look after her. She seemed not to see them, but Jules did, and he felt very proud to be her escort. She looked very pretty in her tight-fitting black jacket and little hat tipped with fur, her cheeks scarlet with the early frost. She was the last person in the crowd, Jules thought, who would be taken for an acrobat. It seemed to him wonderful that she should appear so unlike the marvel that she was, and this lack of resemblance to herself made her the more attractive to him.

After that day, Jules went to church with Mademoiselle Blanche every Sunday. At first the sight of the priests in their vestments, of the altar-boys in their white surplices, of the white altar gleaming with candles and plate and enshrouded in incense, and the reverberation of the organ, mingled with the voices singing the music of the mass, all reminded him so strongly of his mother, that his old affection for her swept over him, and brought tears to his eyes.

His own disbelief had made him doubt even the faith of others. It had also inspired him with the hatred for priests, so common even among Parisians of traditions like his own. Now, as he watched them, chanting at the altar, they seemed harmless as other men. He tried, as he went mechanically through the service, to count the men he knew who went to church. Nearly all of his acquaintances, he found, scoffed at it. Then gradually the service became subtly mingled with his love for the girl beside him, and for her sake he loved it. The organ seemed to sing her praise exultingly. He would have liked to tell her of this fancy, but he did not dare; he knew it would shock her. In a short time, going through the mass with her grew to mean to him an expression of his love, a spiritual exaltation which he offered as a tribute, not to God, but to her.

Chapter VII

By the month of November, Jules had identified himself with Madame Perrault and her daughter. He took his position as their friend and recognized escort so quickly and so quietly that he was himself surprised by it. There were moments when he had a fear that it was all an illusion, that some night he should find the stage-door of the *Cirque* slammed in his face.

It was while watching Mademoiselle Blanche in the ring that he found it most difficult to realize his happiness. He actually *knew* this wonderful creature in white tights who darted from trapeze to trapeze, who posed like a marble statue on the rope, who shot through the air like a thunderbolt! He saw her every day; he loved her, and she knew that he loved her. Sometimes he fancied that she loved him in return—from an expression in her face, a glance of her eyes, a blush, a tremor when his hand touched hers. He did not dare speak to her about his love; he doubted if he should ever dare to speak; at a word he feared his happiness might be shattered.

Sometimes on Sunday afternoons he drove with Mademoiselle Blanche and her mother into the country, and on Sunday nights he would dine and pass the evening with them in the little apartment. Occasionally he had long talks with the mother; in these he told about his family and about his property, laying stress on the fact that even if he lost his place at the office his income was large enough to support him. She told him, in return, about her own family and her husband's, and gave him a humorous account of her sister-in-law, Blanche's Aunt Sophie.

"Blanche is a little like her," she said. "Sophie takes everything *au grand sérieux*. Then she's strict with the children, and that's a great mistake, for Jeanne hates restraint, and Louise doesn't need it."

She also told him amusing stories about Monsieur Berthier's devotion to her. He had offered himself to her while she was at the convent where she was educated, near Boulogne, and she had refused him twice. Her family had objected to her marriage with Blanche's father, simply because he was an acrobat. No, she hadn't fallen in love with him at the circus. She never saw him perform till a short time before she became engaged to him. Ah, it had been hard for her to be separated from him so much. Sometimes she travelled with him in his long journeys; but while the children were very young, she couldn't. Blanche had been such a consolation to him. Madame

Perrault believed that husband and wife ought never to be separated; it was bad for both of them. If she had her life to live over again, she would always travel with her husband, no matter how far he went.

Most of Jules' talk with Madame Perrault, however, consisted of a discussion of the qualities of her daughter, whose praises she constantly sang for him. Blanche's ambition, she said, was to provide dowries for her sisters; she had already accumulated a few thousand francs, and these she had set aside for the girls. She never seemed to think that she herself needed a *dot*. Ah, sometimes Madame was very much worried about her daughter's future. Blanche could not marry any of the other performers; they were not worthy of her, and their coarseness and roughness shocked her. Of course, they were good enough in their way, but their way was not Blanche's way.

Then, as Madame became more familiar with Jules, she also grew more confidential. Yes, Blanche had had a great many admirers. The young Prince of Luperto had fallen desperately in love with her in Bucharest three years before, and he had followed her all over Europe. But she had refused to notice any of his letters,—and oh, *mon Dieu!* such letters! Madame had read every one of them, and she had met the Prince the night he tried to force himself into Blanche's dressing-room. He seemed *such* a gentleman, and he had the most beautiful eyes! But Blanche,—she was so frightened. She cried and cried, and for weeks she was in terror of her life! Then there were others,—so many, so many. One by one, Madame Perrault unfolded their histories to Jules, and he listened in rapt attention, with a growing appreciation of the daughter's charms and of the mother's amiability.

Jules often wondered why he did not hear more talk about the circus in the little apartment. The subject was rarely mentioned. Mademoiselle Blanche displayed no nervousness before or after her performance. She practised a little in the morning at home, she said, to keep her muscles limber; she had done the same things on the trapeze so often that they had become easy to her. Once Jules met in the apartment the oily little Frenchman who always held the rope when Mademoiselle Blanche climbed to the top of the *Cirque*, and then he learned for the first time that Monsieur Pelletier was Mademoiselle's agent. "And he is such a trial to us," the mother explained when he was gone. "He makes such bad terms, and we have to pay him such a high percentage; and then he sometimes mixes up our dates, and we don't know what to do. Ah, if we could only have some one to take care of our affairs that we could trust. It is so hard for two unprotected women."

Jules thought of this speech many times. Indeed, he fairly brooded over it. For several weeks he had felt that his career was too limited; he hated the thought of being tied down to his business all his life. He was made for something better than that, for a grander, a more conspicuous *rôle*.

In his youth he had thought of the army, then of a diplomatic career; for a time, too, of the stage. But he had been too poor to enter either of the first two professions, and for the stage he was unfitted by temperament. Now, in his imagination a brilliant career stretched before him, combining both glory and love. Up to the present he had not lived; his life was about to begin. The world seemed to open out to him! He would travel from one end of the earth to the other in an unbroken march of triumph. Even Paris lost attractiveness for him and seemed uninteresting and petty; he pitied the poor *boulevardiers* who were bound to a wretched routine of existence, who loved it simply because they knew of no other. He would not only visit America again—this time not in a sordid capacity, friendless and lonely, but surrounded by a retinue—he would go also to Russia, to India, to Australia, perhaps to Japan and the other countries of the remote East. The night when he was first enchanted by this vision, he could not sleep for excitement till nearly four o'clock. Then he saw the vision realized, only to be shattered by Madeleine's cracked voice, and her injunction that it was time for him to get up and go to his work.

In the evening, when he saw his friends again, he found them very unhappy; they had just received news from Jeanne that Aunt Sophie was very ill, threatened with pneumonia. Madame Perrault was in tears, and Mademoiselle Blanche's eyes showed that she, too, had been crying. The next day, they said, Jeanne had promised to write, and the next night Jules learned that bad news had been received. The doctor pronounced the case pneumonia, and said the patient was in great danger. Mamma must come on, Jeanne wrote. But Madame explained to Jules with sobs that she could not leave Blanche.

"And my poor Jeanne, what will she do, a child of fourteen with only the little Louise to help her."

Then Jules became inspired. His faithful Madeleine—she would save the situation. Madame Perrault might go to Boulogne by the first train, and Madeleine would take her place, would be a second mother to Mademoiselle Blanche, accompany her to the theatre, help her to dress, come back with her, keep her from being lonely. Jules wanted to rush off at once, and bring Madeleine to the *rue St. Honoré,* for inspection and approval.

Then the girl's quiet wisdom asserted itself. Jeanne had said there was no immediate danger; so if Mamma took the train in the morning, that would be in quite time enough. After their *petit déjeuner* they might call on Madeleine, or Monsieur Jules might tell them if she would come. Then Jules burst into a eulogy of Madeleine's qualities: he had never before realized what a good soul she was. He would bring her with him, he said, in the morning, on his way to the office; he knew she would be glad to come.

On this occasion Jules had a chance to display his executive ability. After leaving his friends at the Circus, he drove home furiously, found Madeleine sound asleep in the big chair by the fireplace, woke her up, and explained the situation.

"Now, my dear Madeleine," he said at the end, "you are to go to that poor girl and take her mother's place; she will love you, and you will love her. So be good to her for my sake, Madeleine," and he leaned over, and patted the old woman's wrinkled hand affectionately. Madeleine was moved, chiefly, however, by Jules' unwonted tenderness. She had never known an actress, not to speak of a performer in a circus, and she felt alarmed at the thought of meeting one. But she felt sure that Mademoiselle Blanche must be good. Hadn't Jules said so? Jules had not said that he was in love with Mademoiselle; he trusted Madeleine to find that out for herself; he also trusted Madeleine to find out a few other things for him. Secretly he was blessing the chance that enabled him to send Madeleine to Mademoiselle; for the moment he did not even think of the personal discomfort it would cause himself.

That night Jules told his friends that Madeleine had consented to come, and he promised to bring her with him in the morning. Madeleine was greatly agitated, and rose unusually early to make an elaborate toilette. She rarely went out, save to the shops and to mass; so she had not kept up with the fashions, and her best dress was made in a mode long before discarded. She was a very grotesque figure as she walked in her queer little bonnet with long ribbons flying from it, and her wide skirts. When they reached the apartment in the *rue St. Honoré,* Jules thought he saw an expression of amusement in Madame Perrault's face, but Blanche greeted Madeleine with great kindliness. Then the mother explained that she had just received a letter from Jeanne, saying Aunt Sophie was in no immediate danger, but begging her to come as soon as possible. Jules saw that both his friends were pleased with Madeleine, and it was quickly arranged that she should install herself in the apartment that day, and at four o'clock Madame Perrault would leave for Boulogne. He departed radiantly happy, with the promise to return at three to take Madame to the station. He secured leave of absence from the office, and on his return to the apartment he found Madeleine there, helping Mademoiselle Blanche to make a new dress.

"I'll be ready in a minute," Madame Perrault cried from the adjoining room.

"Are you coming with us, mademoiselle?" Jules asked.

"No, I won't let her," her mother replied. "It's too cold, and it would tire her. You aren't afraid to ride alone in a cab with me, are you?"

Jules was surprised by her vivacity; he knew that she was greatly worried about her sister, yet in the midst of her agitation she could joke. If he had known her less he would have supposed that she was a woman of little feeling. She presently flounced out of the room, putting on her gloves and smiling.

"Madeleine and Blanche have become great friends," she said. "I'm afraid I shall be jealous of her. When I come back there won't be any place for me." Then she took her daughter by both hands and Jules saw the glimmer of tears in her eyes. "Good-bye, dear," she said, kissing the girl on both cheeks. "You must write to me every day, and I'll write to you. In a week, at least, I shall be back. I have a presentiment that Sophie will improve as soon as I get there."

Mademoiselle Blanche clung tightly to her mother, and kissed her again and again.

"There, there! Now, my child—there!" With a parting embrace, Madame Perrault tore herself away, crying as she passed out of the door, "Good-bye, Madeleine. Take care of the little one! And remember Monsieur Jules is coming back to dinner. I'm going to invite him."

This was the first time she had ever called Jules by his first name, and on hearing it he felt a thrill of joy. She hurried before him down the steep stairs, wiping her eyes. When they entered the cab, she had controlled herself again, and was smiling as usual.

The cab rattled so noisily over the pavement that during most of the ride to the station they kept silent. They arrived there half an hour ahead of time, and this they spent in walking up and down the platform.

"You must be very kind to my Blanche while I'm away," said Madame Perrault. "She will be very lonely. She hasn't been separated from me before since her father died."

Jules assured her that he would be a second mother to her. He would take her and Madeleine to the *Cirque* every night, and in the morning on his way to the office he would call to ask if he could do her any service. "She'll be spoiled when you come back," he concluded with a smile.

For a moment they walked without speaking. The station was so cold that their breaths made vapour in the air. Yet Jules felt warm enough; his whole being seemed to glow.

"There's something I want to tell you."

She made a sign with her head that she was listening.

"I'm in love with Mademoiselle Blanche," he said, impressively, finding a delicious relief in speaking the words.

She smiled roguishly into his face.

"Is that all?"

They looked into each other's eyes, and read there a mutual understanding.

"Then you've known all along?"

"Of course, from the very first, from the first night you came into the dressing-room, and pretended to be a reporter."

"Ah, I thought you had forgiven that."

"So I have—that is, there was nothing to forgive. You didn't deceive me."

"Do you mean that you knew at the time I wasn't a reporter? And Blanche—she knew too?"

"No, poor dear, she didn't know. Yet it was plain as daylight. Ah, my friend, I haven't lived fifty years for nothing. Don't you suppose I could tell from your looks and your manner, and what you said, and what you *didn't* say,—don't you suppose I could tell from all that, what you had come for?"

Jules looked into her face again.

"How good you are!" he sighed.

She burst out laughing.

"Good? I am not good. Blanche taught me that years ago. There's nothing like having a good daughter to take a mother down. She makes me feel ashamed every day of my life."

"That's just the way she makes me feel," Jules cried, delighted to find that some one else shared his feeling. "Then she's so gentle and so kind," he rhapsodized, "and she thinks so little about herself! Do you—do you think——Oh, that's what almost drives me to despair sometimes. I hardly dare go near her. I hardly dare to speak to her."

Madame Perrault took a deep breath.

"You almost make me feel young again," she said, with a smile.

"Do you think I could make her love me?" Jules asked, marvelling at his own humility.

"Do you mean that you want to know whether I think she's in love with you or not?" Madame Perrault said briskly. "Ah, my friend, I can't answer that question. You must ask her yourself."

"Then you give me permission to ask her? You are willing? You have no objection?" He stopped suddenly, and looked radiantly at Madame Perrault's face. "How *good* you are, madame!" he repeated.

She began to laugh again,—a peculiar, gurgling laugh that came from her throat.

"Why should I object? You are a good fellow. You would make Blanche a good husband. It's time for her to get married. She needs some one to protect her. I can't follow her about all the rest of my life. She is twenty-two. Why shouldn't she marry?"

Jules' ardor was cooled by this practical reasoning; it made him practical too. He told Madame Perrault again of his little property. He could well afford to marry, he said. He loved Mademoiselle Blanche with all his heart; he couldn't live without her; he would give up everything for her; he would follow her everywhere. Ah, if he only knew whether she cared for him or not! She was so strange, so reserved. It was so hard to tell with a girl like her.

"You are right there, my friend. She has great reserve. With my Jeanne or Louise, I should know everything. But with Blanche, *non!* But I never pry into her secrets; I have learned better. She has a great deal of inner life; she thinks a great deal; she is not like the other flighty women that you see in the circus. If she had not been born to the circus, if she had been brought up as Louise has been, she would be a *religieuse*."

Jules would have become rhapsodical again if the whistle of the train had not sounded, and he was obliged hurriedly to help Madame Perrault into her compartment. He shook the hand that she offered him, received a few last messages, and he watched the train as it pulled out of the station. Then, with a sigh, he turned and walked back to his office.

Chapter VIII

After the departure of Madeleine, Jules would have found his apartment cheerless, if he had not used it merely for sleeping. As soon as he rose in the morning, he went to Madame Perrault's, where he breakfasted with Mademoiselle Blanche. In spite of her duties elsewhere, Madeleine kept his rooms in order, and his new domestic arrangements did not in the least inconvenience him. Indeed, he liked them, and he almost dreaded the return of Mademoiselle's mother. This would probably not take place for several weeks, however, for the illness of her aunt Sophie proved to be very tedious, though after the first ten days she was pronounced out of danger. Madeleine had speedily won the affections of Mademoiselle Blanche, and she secretly confided to Jules that the girl was an angel.

"I knew you'd think so," Jules replied. "I've thought so ever since I first saw her."

"Ah, but it's wicked that she should have to do those dreadful things every night!" Madeleine cried, rolling her eyes, and throwing up her hands in horror. "It freezes my blood."

"But she likes it," Jules explained.

"Ah, it's wicked just the same, the poor child!"

Madeleine had speedily adapted herself to her duties as dresser to Mademoiselle Blanche, and her nightly trips to the theatre were the most exciting experiences of her life. After seeing the plunge from the top of the Circus, however, she had refused to look at it again. "It freezes my blood," she would repeat, whenever Jules referred to it. "It's too horrible!"

"But she makes a lot of money by it," Jules insisted.

"She would do much better to stay poor," Madeleine replied, with a tartness that was rare with her and made Jules burst out laughing.

"Madeleine," he said, confidentially. "Madeleine, come over here."

Madeleine bent her head towards him with a smile on her face.

"Madeleine, do you think there's any one—any one that she cares about particularly—any one you know? Eh?"

Madeleine's wrinkles deepened, as the smile spread over her face and lighted her faded eyes.

"Ah, Monsieur Jules, she is very fond of her sisters. She is always talking about them, especially about *la petite* Jeanne. Then she's very fond of her mamma, too, of course."

"Madeleine, you're trying to plague me now. You know I don't mean that. I mean any—any—?"

"Any gentleman, Monsieur Jules?" the old woman asked.

"Yes, Madeleine, any gentleman."

Madeleine grew thoughtful.

"She often speaks of Monsieur Berthier, who is going to marry her mother. She says he's very kind to her sisters."

"And is that all, Madeleine? Doesn't she speak of any one else? Doesn't she ever speak of—of me?"

"Oh, yes, Monsieur Jules, she thinks you've been very good to her and her mother. She often speaks of that."

This was all the information that Jules could extract from Madeleine. On several occasions he tried her again, but though she seemed amused by his questions, she evaded them. Once he said to her:

"Madeleine, how would you like to go away with me—to travel—a long distance?"

Madeleine carefully considered the question. Then she replied simply:

"I should not like to leave Paris, Monsieur Jules, but, if you wanted me to go, I would go."

After that, Madeleine was less worried. She had little to say, and, like most silent people, she observed and thought a great deal. For Mademoiselle Blanche she had conceived a genuine affection, and she looked forward with regret to the time when she would have to leave the *rue St. Honoré* for Jules' lonely apartment.

One Saturday night, on their return from the Circus, Jules asked Mademoiselle Blanche if she were going to high mass the next day as usual. He was surprised when she replied that she was going at eight o'clock instead.

"But that is too early," he said. "You won't have sleep enough."

"I'm going to communion," she explained.

"Oh!"

He could not understand why this announcement should impress him as it did. He had supposed that of course she went to communion; she had probably gone to confession early in the afternoon before the *matinée*. Once again he felt awed by her goodness. How strange it was that she should be in the confessional at three o'clock, and two hours later perform in her fleshings before a crowd of people! The very publicity of her life seemed to exalt the simplicity and the purity of her character.

Jules was so absorbed in thinking of these things that he did not speak again till the cab reached the *rue St. Honoré*. Then, as he helped Mademoiselle out, he said:

"I'll go to church with you to-morrow, if you will let me. You won't leave before half-past seven, will you?"

She protested that he ought not to get up so early; he needed a good night's rest after his hard work of the week. But he laughed and waved his hand to her in parting, and told her not to wait for him after a quarter to eight; now that he didn't have Madeleine to call him, he might not wake up in time.

He was in time, however, and as he walked to church in the cold December air with Mademoiselle by his side, he felt repaid for his sacrifice. She wore a tight-fitting fur coat and a black cloth dress, with the little fur-trimmed hat he had admired when he first walked with her in the *Champs Élysées*. Her face was protected by a thick dotted veil, but under it he could see her sparkling eyes and the color in her cheeks.

"I'm paying you a very great compliment," he said, as they hurried along towards *St. Philippe de Roule*. "I haven't got up so early on a Sunday since I was a boy."

She smiled in reply; it was too cold for her to speak. He could see her breath steaming faintly through the veil.

He felt a curious desire to hear her voice again; he did not realize that her devotion to the Church made her seem more remote from him, but he had an unpleasant consciousness that his own lack of religious faith created a barrier between them.

In the church he kept glancing from the priest celebrating the mass, to her. She was absorbed in reading her prayer-book, and she did not once look up at him. He compared her as she appeared then with her appearance in the glamor of the circus ring. She was the same person, yet different. She represented to him a kind of miracle. How humble she was, how sweet and good, as she knelt there!

When the priest began to distribute the communion and Blanche left her seat and joined the throng approaching the altar, Jules was touched with a tenderness he had never felt before. He buried his face in his hands, and prayed that he might be made worthy of her. He did not dare pray for her love; a certain sense of shame at having neglected God and church for so many years, at having lived solely for his own gratification, kept him from that; but if he had examined his motives, he would have found that this was really what he was praying for. He deceived himself so easily that he instinctively felt that he might be able to deceive God too.

On leaving the church, Jules proposed that they go to a restaurant for breakfast. "We'll make a holiday of it," he said, "and drink to your Aunt Sophie's health."

But Blanche protested that Madeleine would expect them, and would be worried if she were not back by half-past nine.

"Then we'll go out at one o'clock. I'll take you over to Bertiny's, in the *Champs Élysées*. It's very gorgeous; the twins took me there once to celebrate Dufresne's luck when he won five hundred francs at the races."

Though the sun was shining, it was still very cold, and as they hurried to the little apartment Jules could see that she was trembling. Madeleine had prepared some hot coffee for them and some eggs, and over these they were very gay. Jules was in a particularly good humor, and Mademoiselle Blanche laughed at his jokes, though most of them she had heard before. She had a very pretty laugh, he thought,—like her mother's, though not so deep and gurgling. After breakfast her face flushed from her walk and she looked even prettier than she appeared in the church.

As Madeleine cleared away the table, Blanche began to water the flowers by the window, and Jules opened the copy of the *Petit Journal* that he had bought on the way from the church. He kept glancing up at Mademoiselle, however, and each time he looked at her he had a new sensation of pleasure. How domestic she looked in the little dress of gray wool that she had put on after her return from mass! She seemed to create an atmosphere of home around her. In her belt were the roses he had given her the night before, still fresh and sparkling with drops of water from her fingers. How good it was, he thought, that he could be with her like this! How lonely his own apartment would be to him when Madame Perrault came back! He almost wished that she would never return, that she would marry Monsieur Berthier, and they might go on in this way forever. He laughed at the thought, and just then Mademoiselle turned her head.

"Monsieur seems to be amused," she said. "What is he smiling at?"

"I'm smiling because I'm so happy," Jules replied. "Don't you smile when you're happy?"

She took a seat by the table, where she rested one hand.

"No, I don't think I do," she said, apparently giving the question serious consideration. "When I am very happy I look serious. Then mamma sometimes fancies I feel sad."

He took a cigarette-case from his pocket and began to smoke.

"Do you know," he said at last, "I shall be sorry when your mother returns?"

"Sorry?"

"Yes, because Madeleine will come back to me then, and I shall have to stay at home. I can't come any more as I do now."

A look of alarm appeared in her face. "But why can't you come just the same?" she asked, innocently.

He burst out laughing, and he felt a sudden desire to pat her on the cheek as he might have done to a child. What a child she was, anyway! Yet he would not have wished her to be different; she seemed to him just what a young girl should be.

"When your mother comes, I can't take breakfast with you any more, and I can't come early on Sunday mornings and stay all day. I shall have to go back to my lonely apartment."

"But you have Madeleine," she said, with a faint smile.

"Madeleine, yes, and she is good enough in her way." Then he suddenly threw his cigarette into the fireplace, and bent toward her. "Don't you know," he whispered, in a voice so low that Madeleine, who was moving about in the next room, could not hear him, "can't you see that it's *you* I shall miss? Can't you see that you've become everything in the world to me? Without you, dear Blanche, I shouldn't care to live. Before I met you I didn't know what life really was—I didn't know what love was. I loved you the first time I saw you, and the more I've seen you, the better I've known you, the dearer you've become to me. I don't think I ever really understood what it was to be pure and good till I knew you. You've made me ashamed of myself. Sometimes I feel as if I had no right to go near you. But I do love you, Blanche, and they say love helps a man to be good. I haven't dared to tell you this before; I've been afraid to ask you if you loved me. But this morning in church, it all came over me so—so that I must tell you. Blanche," he went on, taking her hand, "you aren't offended with me for saying this, are you? I love you so much—I can't help loving you. If you'll only love me a little, dear, I'll be satisfied. Won't you tell me if you do care for me a little—just a little?"

He knelt by her side, and tried to look into her face; but she turned her head away, and he saw that her neck was crimson. Her bosom kept rising and falling convulsively. Then he pressed toward her and clasped her in his arms and kissed her again and again,—on the face, the forehead, the hair, even on her ears when she buried her head on his shoulder. His lips were wet with her tears, and he felt radiantly, exultantly happy.

"I love you, I love you!" he kept repeating.

For the first time he felt sure that his love was returned; but he was not satisfied. He wanted to hear her speak out her love. His lips were on her cheek, and she was lying motionless in his arms, as he whispered:

"Won't you say that you love me, dear? Just three words. That isn't much, and it will make me the happiest man that ever lived."

Instead of speaking, she put her arms on his shoulders, as a child might have done, and he pressed her close to his breast again. Then he heard a noise behind him, and he saw Madeleine standing, big-eyed, in the doorway; she seemed too startled to move. He rose quickly to his feet, and still holding Blanche's hand, he said:

"Madeleine, come here!"

She came forward timidly, as if afraid she might be punished for her intrusion.

"Mademoiselle Blanche is going to be my wife, Madeleine."

Madeleine held out her arms to the girl, and for a moment they stood clasped in each other's embrace.

"Ah, Monsieur Jules," the old woman cried, "I pray God your mother can look down from heaven and see what a good daughter she's getting!"

Chapter IX

After confessing his love, Jules experienced, mingled with his exultation, a feeling of bewildered amazement at his own boldness. This was followed by a poignant regret that he hadn't spoken before. Now, however, that his weeks of doubt and of intermittent misery were over, he gave himself up to his happiness, which manifested itself in a wild exuberance of spirits.

In a short time he was speaking humorously of those weeks, ridiculing himself as if he had already become different, almost another person from what he had been then. He told Blanche about his tortures, and even succeeded in extorting a confession from her that she had been in love with him since the first Sunday when he had called at the apartment and acknowledged Durand's duplicity; she, too, had had her doubts and her fears. Then they became very confidential, and by the time the morning was over, and they found themselves in the restaurant, they felt as if they had known each other intimately for years.

In spite of Blanche's protests, Jules ordered a bottle of champagne and an elaborate luncheon.

"I suppose I ought to have asked Madeleine to come," he said, "but I wanted to be alone with you. Some day before your mother returns, we'll have another *fête*, and take Madeleine with us."

In the morning, when he spoke about a definite engagement, and she protested that her mother must be consulted, he had told her of his talk with Madame Perrault at the railway station. Now he went on to make plans for their marriage. There was no reason, he argued, why they should wait a long time; her mother had been engaged to Monsieur Berthier for three years, but she would not marry till Blanche had a protector. Jules liked to talk of himself in this character; it gave him a feeling of importance. So, altogether, he went on, the sooner the marriage took place the better. He would give up his place in the wool-house, and devote himself to his wife's career; for, of course, they couldn't be separated. They would be very happy travelling about, from one end of the world to the other.

It never occurred to either of them that Blanche might retire from the ring after marriage. She herself seemed to regard the circus as part of her life; she had been born in it, and she belonged to it as long as she was able to perform. As for Jules, he could not have dissociated her from the thought of the circus. Even now he felt as if he had himself become wedded to it, that he had acquired a kind of proprietary interest in it. He discussed Blanche's professional engagements as if they were his own. Why, he asked, couldn't the marriage take place during the weeks that intervened between her engagement at the *Cirque Parisien* and her appearance in Vienna? Jeanne and Louise could come up to Paris for Christmas and the New Year, and be present at the ceremony. By that time he would have his affairs arranged so that he could go with her to Vienna.

Of course, they must dismiss Pelletier after their marriage. Jules would take charge of his wife's affairs; his capacity for business would enable him to make good terms for her. He would plan wonderful tours; he would write to America, perhaps, and secure engagements for her there; artists were wonderfully well paid in America, better than in any other country, and they would enjoy seeing the new world together.

Blanche listened to his talk with a touching confidence; she seemed to think it natural that he should speak as if he had authority over her. She made no protest against any of his suggestions, though she repeated that nothing could be decided till her mother returned to Paris.

"But we'll write to your mother," said Jules. "We'll write to her this very day—this afternoon when we go back."

For a moment her face clouded.

"What's the matter? Don't you want me to write to your mother?"

She did not reply at once. When she did speak, she kept her eyes fixed on her plate.

"It will be so hard to be separated from her."

Jules laughed, and bent toward her.

"But you can't stay with her always," he said tenderly. "Then we'll take Madeleine with us. That will be a capital plan. She's strong and healthy, though she's over sixty, and she won't mind the travelling. Besides, we shall be in Vienna three months, and we'll rent a little apartment. It will be like being at home."

He spoke as if their future were settled, and his tone of confidence seemed to reassure her.

"I should like to have Madeleine," she said simply. "She is so good."

On their return to the apartment, they devoted themselves to writing long letters to Madame Perrault. Jules' letter was full of rhapsodies, of promises to be kind to the girl who had consented to be his wife, and of his plans for the future. They read their letters to each other, or rather Jules read all of his, and Blanche read part of hers, firmly refusing to allow him to hear the rest. They spent a very happy afternoon together, and in the evening Madeleine had a sumptuous dinner for them, with an enormous bunch of fresh roses on the table. In the evening they went to the *Comédie Française*, to finish what Jules declared to be the happiest day of his life.

Jules counted that day as the beginning of his real career. He looked back on himself during the years he had lived before it almost with pity. Since leaving the *lycée*, he had been merely a drudge, a piece of mechanism in the odious machinery of business. He had been content enough, but with the contentment of ignorance. How lonely and sordid his existence out of the office had been! He thought of his solitary dinners in *cafés*, surrounded by wretched beings like himself deprived of the happiness that comes from home and from an honest love. To the twins and his other comrades at the office he said nothing of the change that had taken place in his life; he was afraid they would chaff him; of course, when they heard he was going to marry an acrobat, they would make foolish jokes and treat him with a familiar levity. He determined not to tell them of his marriage until the eve of his departure from business; he would have to give the firm at least a fortnight's notice; but he would merely explain to Monsieur Mercier that he intended to devote a few months to travel, and thought of going to America.

Madame Perrault replied at once to Jules' letter. She made no pretence of being surprised by the news it contained; and she expressed her pleasure at the engagement, and gave her consent. But they must not make any definite plans until her return to Paris. That would be in about two weeks, for Aunt Sophie was very much better now and rapidly gaining strength, though she had as yet been unable to leave her bed. As soon as Sophie could go out, she was to be carried to the house of her cousin, Angélique Magnard, who would give her the best of care. Then Madame Perrault would be able to take Jeanne and Louise to Paris for the holidays; the girls were wild to see their dear Blanche again and to meet Jules. Monsieur Berthier talked of coming with them; he, too, was eager to make the acquaintance of Blanche's future husband.

After these preliminaries, Madame Perrault devoted herself to practical matters. She felt it her duty to inform Monsieur Jules that Blanche had no *dot*; she had earned a great deal of money, but most of it had been spent in maintaining the family; since the death of her father she had been their sole support. Of course, after marriage, her daughter's earnings would belong to Jules; but he must distinctly understand that he was taking a penniless bride. After her own marriage, Madame Perrault would have no fear for the future; Monsieur Berthier had promised of his own accord to provide for the girls; indeed, it was chiefly for their sake that, at the age of fifty-three, she was willing to marry again. So Blanche would no longer have her family dependent on her.

Jules replied with an impassioned letter. He didn't care whether Blanche had a *dot* or not. He wanted to marry her because he loved her, because without her his life would be unendurable: he would marry her if she were the poorest girl in France. It took him several pages to say this, and he read the letter with satisfaction, and then aloud to Blanche, who laughed over it, and gave him a timid little kiss in acknowledgment of his devotion. He thought he had done a commendable act, and he felt convinced that every word he had written was true.

At the office Jules grew reserved, and he resented haughtily the familiarities of the twins. Indeed, to all of his companions in the wool-house he could not help displaying the superiority he felt. He would be there only a few weeks longer, and he acted as if he were conferring a favor on his employer by staying. The twins spent many hours in discussing the change in him; but they could not discover the cause.

"You ought to have heard him talk to old Mercier the other day," said Leroux. "You'd think he was the President receiving a deputation."

Early in November, Blanche received a letter from her mother, saying Aunt Sophie was so much better that they had decided to move her the next day, and two days later she would herself leave Boulogne with the girls and Monsieur Berthier. Jules was both glad and sorry to hear the news,—sorry because his long *tête-à-têtes* with Blanche would end for a time, and glad because he would be able to arrange definitely with her mother for the marriage. Madeleine grieved at parting with the girl, but was consoled when Jules explained that she would probably be needed every night at the circus after Madame Perrault's return, for, of course, Monsieur Berthier would want to take his *fiancée* to the theatres. In speaking of Monsieur Berthier, Jules had adopted a facetious tone, which half-amused and half-pained Blanche.

"How droll it will be," he said one day, "to have two pairs of lovers billing and cooing together."

"Mamma doesn't bill and coo," the girl replied, with just a suggestion of resentment in her tone. "She's too sensible." Then Jules patted her affectionately on the cheek, and told her she mustn't take what he said so seriously.

"Monsieur Berthier must be a very good man, or he wouldn't get such a good wife," he said lightly. Then, with a comic look in his eyes, he added as an afterthought: "What a very good person I must be!"

The next night, when Jules appeared in the *rue St. Honoré* for dinner, he found the little apartment crowded. Madame Perrault embraced him, and by addressing him as "my son," seemed to receive him formally into the family. Then she introduced the two girls, who were much larger than he had imagined them to be. Jeanne, rosy-cheeked and black-eyed, approached him fearlessly, and offered her hand with a smile; Louise, fair and slight, with her light brown hair braided down her back, looked frightened, and blushed furiously when she received her salutation. The little fat man standing in front of the mantel, Jules recognized at once from his pointed white beard and laughing eyes.

"I should have known you in a crowd on the *Boulevard*," Jules said, as he extended his hand. "You're exactly like your photograph."

"And you are even better-looking than Mathilde said you were," Monsieur Berthier replied. "Ah, little one," he went on, turning to Blanche, and giving her a pinch on the arm, "you're getting a fine, handsome husband."

Jules tried to make friends with the girls. With Jeanne he had no difficulty; she was quite ready to banter with him, and he found her pert and quick-witted. Louise, however, was so shy that he could extract only monosyllables from her. She seemed to him very like Blanche, only less pretty. Jeanne had Blanche's beauty, more highly-colored and exuberant; her snapping black eyes showed, too, that she had a will and a temper of her own. Jules began to chaff her, to make her show her spirit, but she parried his jests good-humoredly, and she retaliated very smartly.

"I don't see how you ever dared to fall in love with Blanche," she said. "Aren't you afraid of her?"

"Afraid of her?" Jules laughed. "Why should I be afraid of her?"

"Oh, I don't know. I suppose because she's so good. I'm afraid of her sometimes. And I'm afraid of Louise when she gets her pious look on. How did you happen to fall in love with her? Do tell me. I'll never tell in the world."

"I just saw her, that's all," Jules explained with mock gravity. "Isn't that enough?"

"In the circus?"

Jules nodded.

"Then you fell in love with her because she does such wonderful things, and looks so beautiful in the ring. Now, you wouldn't have fallen in love if you'd just met her like any one else."

"But it was because she wasn't like anyone else that I did fall in love with her," Jules insisted, with the air of carrying on the joke.

"But if she'd never been in the circus—if you'd just met her here, or anywhere else except in the circus—do you think you would have fallen in love with her then?"

"Of course I should," Jules replied unhesitatingly, though he knew he was lying.

Jeanne shrugged her shoulders and looked skeptical.

"I wish I could be in the circus," she said, "and get flowers, and be admired, and earn a lot of money like Blanche. And isn't it the funniest thing," she went on, growing more confidential, "Blanche doesn't care about it at all."

"About the flowers, and being admired, and all that?"

"Yes. And she says the circus isn't a good place for a young girl. But I say if it's good enough for her, it's good enough for me. Anyway, if mamma doesn't let me do what Blanche does, I'm going on the stage when I grow up."

Jules was amused by her talk, and drew her out by deft questions. While she was animatedly describing her life in the convent of Boulogne, where the nuns were always holding up Louise as a model of good behavior to her, dinner was announced, and they all went out into the dining-room, where Jules and Blanche had passed so many hours together. This time Jules' place was between Jeanne and Louise. Jeanne went on with her chatter, and Louise scarcely spoke, save to Blanche, with whom she kept exchanging affectionate smiles.

"The girls are vexed with me," said Madame Perrault, "because I won't let them go to the Circus to-night."

The pale face of Louise brightened with eagerness and Jeanne turned to her mother and cried pleadingly:

"Oh, I think it's a shame. The first time we've been in Paris, too, and we want to see Blanche perform again so much! Why can't we go, mamma? Please, please let us go."

"Oh, let the children go," said Monsieur Berthier good-naturedly. "It would be cruel to send them to bed early their first night in Paris."

Then Jules added his voice in the girls' behalf, but Madame Perrault shook her head decidedly.

"I can't have them up so late. Besides, they need to rest after their journey. If you are good, Jeanne, and don't tease me to go to-night, I'll take you and Louise to the *matinée* on Saturday."

"Oh, the *matinée*!" Jeanne pouted, turning for sympathy to Jules. "Who cares for the *matinée*! Isn't it too bad?" she went on in a low voice, so that her mother shouldn't hear her. "When I grow up, Monsieur Jules, I shall go to the theatre every night—yes, every night of my life. I don't care what happens."

Jeanne was sullen and Louise looked sad when they were left alone with Charlotte, the little maid.

"I won't go to bed till twelve o'clock," Jeanne cried, as her mother, with parting injunctions, went out, followed by the others. "I shall sit up and cry all the evening."

"Nine o'clock, my dear," said Madame Perrault serenely. "You know what I said about Saturday."

The door was slammed behind them and, as they filed downstairs, they heard Jeanne go stamping back into the *salon*.

"Don't you think you're severe with the child, Mathilde?" said Berthier.

"No, Félix, not too severe, if you mean that. It's the only way to keep her in check. She has too much spirit. I'm afraid of it sometimes."

"That's just the way you used to be at her age," he laughed.

"And that's just why I mean to keep her down," she replied, almost sternly.

"Jeanne has all the spirit of the family," said Berthier, glancing at Jules.

After the performance they returned to the apartment for supper. Jules was surprised to find the table steaming with hot dishes, bright with flowers and with wine-glasses. Madeleine, who seemed to be in the secret, put on an apron, and proceeded to assist Charlotte.

"We've prepared a little feast for you," Madame Perrault explained, "in honour of Blanche's engagement. Félix has provided the champagne."

Berthier rubbed his hands and smiled, and they took their places at the table. They were all hungry and in good spirits. This was the happiest time of the day for Blanche; though she never consciously worried about her work, she always felt relieved when her performance was done, and she was free to go home and rest. The little rosy-cheeked Charlotte busied herself around them, passing dishes and bringing on fresh ones.

"It's a shame to keep this poor child up so late," said Berthier, when she had left the room for a moment. "Why not send her to bed?"

"I'll send her as soon as she brings in the rest of the things," Madame Perrault replied. "She and Madeleine can have something to eat together. I sha'n't have to send Madeleine home with you to-night, Jules. We've made a bed for her in Charlotte's room. She's a good creature, your Madeleine."

Charlotte came in with the rest of the dishes, and Madame Perrault told her to eat something, and go to bed. "And tell Madeleine not to wait up for us. You can clear the things away in the morning. Did Jeanne go to bed at nine o'clock, Charlotte?"

"Yes, madame."

"And without any trouble?"

"Yes, madame."

"What did she do to amuse herself during the evening?"

Charlotte's cheeks took on a deeper red.

"She tried to imitate Mademoiselle Blanche in the circus," she confessed.

"Ah, that accounts for the broken chair! Good night, Charlotte." Then, as the girl left the room, Madame Perrault sighed. "That Jeanne will be the death of me."

"I'll take her in hand when she comes to me," Berthier laughed. "We'll have to find a husband for her. That will cure her of her craze for the circus."

"A husband for Jeanne, little Jeanne!" Madame Perrault exclaimed in horror. "She's barely fourteen."

"And in two years she'll be a woman. I was in love with you at fifteen. Don't you remember? We thought of eloping."

"*Taisez-vous!*" cried Madame Perrault, flushing, and trying not to join in the laughter that the speech excited from Jules. "You make me a great fool before my daughter and my new son."

"He isn't your son yet," Berthier insisted, to tease her.

"But he will be soon."

"That's just what I wanted you to say!" Jules cried. "The sooner the better. Tomorrow would suit me."

The glasses had been filled with champagne, and Berthier lifted his glass high in the air, crying:

"Let us drink to the *fiancés*! May their marriage be long and their engagement short! Here's health and happiness to them!"

They all stood up smiling and drank together. Then as they sat down again, Berthier went on:

"Ah, I know the folly of long engagements. Get married, get married, my children, as soon as you can, while love is young. I once knew a young girl—as beautiful as the morning—more beautiful, a thousand times more beautiful. Well, this young girl loved a handsome, yes, I may say a fairly handsome, at any rate, an honest young fellow, who fairly worshipped her in return. But the stern parents of this beautiful young girl— —"

"*Taisez-vous!*" Madame Perrault repeated. "No more nonsense. If your beautiful young girl hadn't obeyed her parents, where would Blanche Perrault be at this moment, I should like to know?"

"Ah, my friend," said Berthier to Jules, "it's the women who forget. Only the men are constant in this world."

Madame Perrault rolled her eyes in mock horror.

"Constant—the men!" she repeated scornfully. "They don't know what constancy is. If it weren't for the constant women in the world, the men would go straight to the devil."

Berthier burst into hilarious laughter. He loved nothing better than to be vanquished in an argument by Madame Perrault. Indeed, he often argued simply in order to provoke her. He gave Jules a quick glance and a nod which plainly said: "Isn't she a fine woman? Have you ever seen a woman so clever?"

The innocent pleasantries of the old lovers, however, were lost on Jules. He wanted to discuss in all seriousness his forthcoming marriage, and this was certainly a suitable occasion. So he determined to put the conversation on another basis.

"I am sure Monsieur Berthier is right about long engagements," he said, "and there's no reason why our engagement shouldn't be short. I love Blanche, and Blanche loves me, and we think we can make each other happy. I can afford to marry—I have a little property—and when she marries me Blanche will have a protector in her professional career."

"Bravo!" cried Berthier. "That was said like a man!"

"And the sooner I'm married, the better for you," Jules went on, fixing his eyes on Berthier's white beard. "Then Madame Perrault won't be tied down to Blanche, and there's no reason why you shouldn't be married, too."

"We might have a double marriage!" said the little man jocosely.

"No, no, *no*!" Madame exclaimed. "When I'm married I shall be married very quietly in Boulogne, without any fuss. These children shall be married first. Then some day, Félix, you and I shall walk to the church and it will be over in five minutes."

Berthier breathed a long sigh, and laid his hand gently on Madame Perrault's arm.

"I've waited a great many years for those five minutes, *chérie*."

"Blanche's engagement at the Circus ends the last day of the year," Jules resumed, "and she begins her season in Vienna on the fifteenth of January. Now, there's no reason in the world that I can think of to prevent our being married between the first of January and the fifteenth."

Then, from every point of view, they discussed the time of the marriage. Madame Perrault raised the question of dresses for the bride, of Jules' inability to arrange his affairs in so short a time, but these and all other objections were overruled.

Blanche herself had very little to say; when her mother asked her point-blank if she wanted the marriage to take place so early, she replied that she was willing if Jules and the others decided it was best. She seemed more like a passive spectator than one actively interested in the discussion; her eyes kept roving from Jules to her mother, and from her mother back to Jules. Berthier supported Jules valiantly, and at two o'clock, Madame Perrault was finally won over, and it was decided that the marriage should take place during the first week in January. Jules kissed Blanche on the cheek, and there was general embracing and laughter. Then the little party broke up, and Monsieur Berthier followed Jules down the stairs.

"Ah, my boy," he said, as they stood on the sidewalk, before saying good-night, "I'd give all the money I've made for your youth. Youth is the time for love. In my youth it came to me, but I lost it. Take good care of it, my friend," he concluded, tapping Jules' hand affectionately as they were about to go their separate ways.

Chapter X

Jules at once began preparations for his marriage. He gave notice of his intention to leave the wool-house, and to move from his apartment. Monsieur Mercier showed no regret at his departure. "I've observed that you were no longer interested in your work," he said coldly.

Jules turned away with a sense of disappointment and pain, feeling that he had been badly treated. Though he said nothing to the twins about his going, they speedily heard of it and gibed him for the reason. He preferred to maintain an air of mystery, but one morning Leroux came into the office, shaking a copy of the *Triomphe* in the air.

"Let me congratulate you!" he cried, extending his hand. "I respect a man that can make a stroke like that. I've known you were up to some game all along," he added insinuatingly.

Jules looked at the paper, and in the column devoted to news of the theatre he read of the engagement of Mademoiselle Blanche, of the *Cirque Parisien*, to Monsieur Jules Le Baron, a young business man of wealth. Dufresne added his congratulations, and one after another during the day Jules' other comrades came up to shake his hand. No wonder he had been putting on airs with them! They treated him very jocosely, however, teased him about his reputed wealth, and tortured him with their coarse jokes, so that he looked forward with relief to escaping from them.

All of Jules' leisure was passed with Blanche and her family. He made friends with the girls and with Monsieur Berthier. The better acquainted he became with Louise the more he liked her; Jeanne sometimes vexed him by making fun of him, though he was careful not to betray his annoyance. For Monsieur Berthier he felt a genuine esteem; the little man was always in good humor, though Jules suspected that, in spite of his success in business, his whole life had been clouded by the disappointment of his youth. As for Madame Perrault, notwithstanding the apparent lightness of her character, which had at first prejudiced him against her, the effective way in which she managed her affairs made him realize that she was a woman to be respected. Sometimes Jules wondered what kind of man Blanche's father had been; he fancied that of the two the mother had been by far the stronger.

Jules passed Christmas with his friends and spent a month's salary on gifts for Blanche and her sisters. For the girls Madame had a *fête* in the morning after mass, with a Christmas tree laden with presents, and decorated with candles and trinkets and *bonbons*. She chose this time of day, as both in the afternoon and evening Blanche gave performances.

The next morning Madame Perrault learned through Pelletier that the circus in Vienna where Blanche had been engaged to appear was a little more than ninety feet high; so the plunge would be fifteen feet deeper than it was in Paris. This news created excitement in the family. It made Madame so nervous that she urged that the engagement be given up and an offer that had come from Nice be accepted; but Jules laughed at the idea.

"What's a difference of fifteen feet to Blanche?" he said. "It's just as easy for her to dive ninety feet as to dive seventy-five. The only thing for Blanche to do is to go to Vienna as soon as her engagement here is over. Then she can practise the plunge every morning for two weeks. We'll simply have to get married a little earlier than we intended."

Madame Perrault saw the force of the argument, and Monsieur Berthier seconded Jules. As for Blanche, she declared that she should not be afraid of the plunge; at Bucharest she had made a plunge of nearly eighty-three feet. So it was agreed that the civil marriage should take place very quietly on the third of January, and the religious ceremony the day after. Jules and his bride could leave Paris by the afternoon train, accompanied by Madeleine. Madame Perrault was anxious to keep any notice out of the papers, if possible; she thought it might injure Blanche professionally. She had been greatly vexed by the paragraph in the *Triomphe* and had attributed it to Durand; but Jules explained that the *Triomphe* was not Durand's paper; besides, the journalist had been sent for the winter to the Riviera as correspondent.

On the last day of the year Jules bade farewell to his associates at the wool-house. Most of them regretted his departure, for before his sudden accession of dignity he had been well liked among them. The next morning, on the first day of his emancipation, when he went to the apartment in the *rue St. Honoré*, he found some pieces of silver there, the gift of his old comrades. He knew at once that the twins had started a subscription for him, and he felt ashamed of his treatment of them during his last weeks among them. He soon forgot about them, however, and was absorbed in the preparations for his new life. He had sold most of his furniture, save a few pieces that were so intimately associated with the memory of his mother that he could not part with them.

For Madeleine this was a trying time; she performed her numerous duties, involving several journeys to the *rue St. Honoré*, with a look of bewilderment in her face, as if she could not adjust herself to the change that was about to take place in her life.

Two days before the time chosen for their civil marriage, Jules was sitting alone with Blanche, beside the fireplace where he had passed most of his courtship. They had been making plans for Vienna, and Jules felt as if he were already at the head of a household.

"Do you know," he said, glancing at the engagement ring on her left hand that sparkled in the firelight, "I haven't been able to make up my mind yet what to give you for a wedding present. I wish you'd tell me what you'd like. I want to give you something that will please you very much."

She looked intently into the fireplace, and did not reply.

"Isn't there something that you want especially?" Then Jules saw her face flush, and he went on quickly: "Ah, I know there is, but you're afraid to tell. Now, out with it. Is it a diamond brooch, or one of those queer little gold watches that women carry, set with jewels, or one of those bracelets that we saw in the shop in the *rue de la Paix* the other day?"

She began to laugh, and without turning her eyes toward him, she said:—

"You know I don't care for those things. But there—there is something—"

"Well, out with it."

"It isn't a—it isn't what you think—a present or anything like that; but it is something I should like to have you—something that would make me very happy."

"Then tell me what it is," said Jules, impatiently. "What are you afraid of? Am I such an ogre?"

For a moment she did not answer. Then she said timidly: "I wish you'd go to confession before we're married."

He burst into a laugh that rang through the apartment.

"Oh, is that all? So you're afraid to marry such a wicked person as I am till the Church has forgiven him and made him good again."

She shook her head.

"No, it isn't that, Jules. I don't believe you are wicked. I don't believe you ever were; but I should be so much happier if you would go to confession, and then before we're married in church we could go to communion together."

He threw himself beside her chair, seized her head in his hands, and kissed her on the forehead. "I'm not fit to be your husband. You're too good for me," he said softly.

She drew away from him with a smile.

"And will it make you very much happier if I go to confession?" he asked.

"Yes, Jules, very much."

For an instant he hesitated, looking into her eyes.

"Then I'll go," he said.

She turned to him, and threw her arms around his neck. As he held her closely to him, his lips pressed against her hair, he went on:—

"But it will be hard for me, Blanche. I haven't been to confession for more than twelve years. Think of all the things I shall have to tell."

"It will be over in a few minutes," she said reassuringly. "Then you'll be glad you've done it."

He rose to his feet and drew his chair nearer hers.

"I've even forgotten how to make a confession. I don't even remember the *Confiteor*."

"Then I shall have to teach it to you. It's in my prayer-book, and you can take it and learn it."

"But I sha'n't know what to do. I shall appear awkward and foolish."

"It's easy enough. You begin by examining your conscience; then you—"

"Examining my conscience! I shall have to wake it up first. It's been sound asleep all these years. Ah, my dear Blanche, you can't imagine how pleasant it is to have your conscience asleep."

She ignored his jesting, and went on: "Then you have to be sorry for what you've done,—for the sins, I mean."

"But if you're not sorry. They've been very pleasant, a good many of them."

"Of course, if you aren't sorry you can't go to confession. That's what people go for, because they *are* sorry, and because they intend to try to be better."

"But all the confessions in the world wouldn't make me better. It's only you that can do that. I'm sorry for my sins simply because, when I think of them, they take me so far away from you. If I hadn't met you, I shouldn't have thought they were so bad. But when I think of you, Blanche, and when I look at you, you seem so good—well, I—I feel ashamed, and then I want to be good too. Why can't I confess to you?" he went on banteringly. "You'd do me more good than all the priests in Christendom. Only I'm afraid I should shock you. I suppose the priests hear stories like mine every day; so one or two more or less wouldn't make any difference to them."

She turned her head away, and he saw that he had offended her. So he patted her cheek and smiled into her face.

"What a little *dévote* she is, anyway! She's vexed even when I joke about her religion. Don't you see that it's all fun, dear? I'm going to do everything you say, make a clean breast of it to the priest, tell him I'm sorry, and promise to be good for the rest of my life. It won't be hard to promise that. How can I help being good when I shall have you with me all the time?"

Then for an hour they talked seriously about the confession. The more he thought of the ordeal, the more nervous Jules felt. Sins came back to him, committed during those first few years after he left the *lycée*, when his freedom was novel and delicious. How could he tell of those things, how could he put them into the awful baldness of speech? He knew that no sin could be concealed in the confessional; but he asked Blanche if he would have to be particular, if he couldn't say in a general way that he had broken this commandment or that. He was alarmed by her reply that she told everything, that sometimes the priest asked probing questions. He couldn't endure the shame of speaking out those horrors. He was afraid, however, to acknowledge his fears to the girl; they might make her suspect what he had done, and inspire her with a loathing for him.

Jules had heard that some men told the women they were going to marry of their lapses, and he had been greatly amused. It never occurred to him that he ought to reveal the dark passages in his life to Blanche; these would simply shock her, give her wrong ideas about him, perhaps make her suspicious and jealous after marriage. His sins he had always regarded as follies of youth: they did not in any way affect his character or his honor as a gentleman. Now, however, he was looking back on himself, not from the point of view of the man of the world, but of a good woman.

That night, on leaving Blanche at the theatre, instead of roaming in the *Boulevards*, or reading the papers in the *cafés*, as he had of late been doing till half-past ten, he took a *fiacre* to the Madeleine, where he spent one of the most disagreeable hours of his life. Vespers were being sung, and the church was nearly full; he sought an obscure corner, knelt there before a picture of Christ carrying the Cross of Calvary, repeated an "Our Father," and a "Hail Mary," which came back to him like an echo of his mother's voice, and then gave himself up to the task of examining his conscience.

The whole panorama of his manhood passed before him, the life of the young Parisian at the close of the century,—selfish, cynical, pleasure-loving, sense-gratifying, animal. He buried his face in his hands. Oh, what an existence! Yet he dared to take a pure young girl for his wife, to make her the mother of his children! He could not think of himself or of his sins without reference to her, and the more he thought of her and of them, the deeper his shame became, and this shame he mistook for contrition. This then was what Blanche had meant by saying that he must be sorry for what he had done, and must promise to fight against temptation. From the depth of his heart he believed he was sorry.

Then he took from his pocket the prayer-book that she had given him, and read several times the act of contrition and the *Confiteor*. The repetition recalled them to his memory, and he was ready for his confession to the priest the next day. With a sigh he rose from his seat, feeling as if he had thrown off the burden of his past life and received a benediction.

The next afternoon, when Jules entered with Blanche the church of *St. Philippe de Roule,* he found groups of people kneeling around the confessional boxes and in front of the altars. He had resolved to confess to Father Labiche, who, Blanche had told him, was the most lenient of all the fathers. The names of the priests were printed on the boxes, and the largest crowd was gathered around the box assigned to Jules' choice.

"I'm afraid you'll have to wait a long time," Blanche whispered.

"Never mind," Jules replied nervously.

He felt almost glad that he was to have a respite. The sight of the confessional boxes and of the people whispering prayers, together with the atmosphere of devotion that pervaded the place, had filled him with terror. Blanche made a sign to him to go forward and join the group awaiting Father Labiche, and she herself stopped near the group beside it, knelt and made the sign of the cross. Jules, too, knelt before one of the hard-wood benches, and prayed that he might have the courage and grace to make a good confession. Then he went over again the sins that he had to confess, and he repeated the *Confiteor* and the act of contrition.

All day long these prayers, and the items of his confession, had been surging in his mind, and now, as he sat up and waited for his turn to come in the procession that passed in and out on either side of the confessional, they kept repeating themselves. He looked at the wrinkled women around him, and wondered if their feelings were like his; he could see no nervousness, no fear in their faces; they seemed to be absorbed, almost exalted in their devotion. Then he began to grow impatient, and wished that the people who entered the confessional would not take so much time. He could catch glimpses of the dark figure of the priest, bending his head from one side to the other, and glancing out at the people. In his line at least fifteen persons were waiting their turn before him; it would take Father Labiche more than two hours, Jules feared, to hear them and the fifteen others in the opposite line. His thoughts turned to Blanche, and he wondered if she had been heard yet. He looked around, and saw her in the crowd behind him, reading her prayer-book; she kept apart from the others, and had evidently finished her confession and was waiting for him.

How gentle and good she looked; how different from her appearance in the ring! Once again he saw her tumbling through the air in her silk tights. He tried to drive this thought from his mind, but again and again he saw her, climbing hand over hand to the top of the Circus, hurling herself backward, spinning through the air, striking the padded net with a thud, bouncing up again, and landing, with the pretty gesture of both hands, on her feet. And in two days she would be his wife! They would go away together, and whenever she performed in public, he would appear with her, hold the rope while she climbed to the top of the building, make the dramatic announcement that would awe the audience into silence, and then scamper across the net to the platform before she fell.

For more than an hour Jules thought of this brilliant future; then he suddenly realized where he was, and he saw that he had moved up within three places of the confessional. In a few moments it would be his turn to go into that dark box, where so many ghastly secrets were told, where he would be obliged to reveal all the vileness and the weakness of his human nature. His nerves vibrated; he felt as if something within him were sinking, as if his courage were leaving him. Then his lips began again to repeat the *Confiteor*, and his mind ran nervously over his self-accusations.

The woman before him remained so long in the confessional that he wondered if she would ever come out; but when she did appear he had a sudden access of terror. He rose mechanically, however, made his way into the box, and knelt beside the little closed slide, through which the priest conferred with the penitents. He could hear the low murmur of Father Labiche's voice, and the more faint responses of a woman confessing on the other side. He tried not to listen, but he could not help catching a few words. Suddenly the slide was opened, and he confronted the kindly face of the old priest whose right hand was raised in blessing.

Blanche had seen Jules enter the confessional, and she waited for him to appear again. The woman who had entered before him on the other side soon came out; so Jules was now making his peace with God. She lowered her head, and breathed a simple prayer of thankfulness. Ten, fifteen minutes passed; still he did not come. She wondered why Father Labiche kept him there so long. When at last he did appear, his face was white. Poor Jules! she thought. How hard it must have been for him, and how good he was to have gone through it so heroically. He walked forward to the main altar, and there he knelt for several moments. When he came back, he found her waiting.

"Come," he said, touching her on the arm.

They did not speak till they were in the street.

"It was pretty tough," he said doggedly. "I thought he'd never let me out."

She smiled up into his face. "But it's all over now, Jules."

"Yes, it's all over," he repeated grimly. "But I should hate to go through it again."

They hurried on through the nipping January air.

"I'm afraid we shall be late for dinner, Jules. It must be after half-past six, and then we have so many things to do to-night. My trunks aren't all packed yet."

"I would help you if I could," Jules replied, "but I must go back to the church. Father Labiche gave me the Stations of the Cross for penance. He said he thought it would do me good before I was married to reflect on the sufferings of Christ," he explained with a smile.

"Then you told him you were going to be married?" she laughed, her breath steaming in the air.

"He asked how I happened to come to confession after staying away so long; so I had to acknowledge that I did it to please you."

The little apartment was in commotion over Blanche's marriage and departure two days later; the *petit salon* was littered with dresses, and the two girls were greatly excited over their new frocks. Jules saw that he was in the way, and soon after dinner he left his friends, saying that he would have the carriages ready for them at half-past seven in the morning; Blanche, her mother, and Monsieur Berthier would ride with him in one, and in the other the girls would go with Madeleine and Pelletier, who had been invited on account of his long business association with the family.

That night at church Jules did his best to put himself into a religious frame of mind and to feel a proper pity for the sufferings of Christ. As he passed from station to station in the Way of the Cross, he reflected seriously on the significance of each, and he said his prayers devoutly. But his mind was constantly distracted by the thought of the girl he loved and of his marriage the next day. At the most inopportune moments visions of Blanche would haunt him as she looked in the ring, climbing the rope and whirling through the air.

When his prayers were said he felt radiantly happy. He had done his duty, and he felt that he deserved to be rewarded. It was only nine o'clock, but he hurried home at once to go on with his packing. When he went to bed that night, he dreamed that he was making his first appearance in the circus at Vienna, holding the rope for his wife, and speaking the thrilling words of warning to the audience.

In the morning Jules and Blanche received communion at early mass, and later they went with Madame Perrault and Monsieur Berthier to the Mayor's office, where the civil marriage ceremony was performed. This Jules regarded merely as a formality, though it made him feel that she was at last his, his forever! No one could take her away from him now! The next morning was clear and cold, and the sun shone as he looked out of his window in the dismantled apartment. He smiled as he thought that his lonely days as a bachelor were over. At ten o'clock he drove to the *rue St. Honoré* with Madeleine, who looked a dozen years younger in her simple black silk with a piece of white lace at her throat, the gift of Madame Perrault. Blanche, in her white satin dress with the bunch of white roses he had sent to her in her hand, had never seemed to him so beautiful. It was after eleven o'clock when they reached *St. Philippe*, and a crowd of idlers hung about the door and followed them into the church.

To Jules the mass that preceded the marriage ceremony seemed interminable; he kept glancing at Blanche's flushed face and downcast eyes, and plucking at his gloves. Then, when he found himself standing before the priest, holding Blanche's hand, and listening to the solemn words of the service, he came near bursting into tears. He thought afterward how ridiculous he would have been if he hadn't been able to control himself. He was relieved when the service was ended, and as he walked to the vestry with his wife on his arm, he could have laughed aloud for joy.

When the register had been signed and they had shaken hands with the priest, they drove at once to the *café* in the *avenue de l'Opéra*, where Jules had ordered a sumptuous breakfast. There they remained till four o'clock. Monsieur Berthier was the gayest of them all, and he was seconded by Jeanne, who pretended to flirt desperately with Jules and made pert speeches to Pelletier. Then they all returned to the *rue St. Honoré*, where Blanche changed her wedding finery for a travelling dress.

During the farewell between Blanche and her family, Jules suffered; he never could bear the sight of women in tears. He was greatly relieved when he put his almost hysterical wife and Madeleine into the carriage, and slammed the door behind him.

Chapter XI

They went straight to Vienna, arriving fatigued from their long journey. After three days, spent at a little French hotel, Jules found near the *Ringstrasse* a furnished apartment that suited him, and they took possession at the end of the week.

Blanche soon felt at home, but Madeleine, though she had become deeply attached to her new mistress, and now had more companionship than she had known since the death of Jules' mother, secretly grieved for her beloved Paris, and looked and acted as if utterly bewildered.

The day of his arrival in Vienna, Jules proceeded to the Circus and had a long talk with Herr Prevost, the manager, with regard to his wife's engagement. He explained the difference in the plunge Blanche would be obliged to take there from her usual one, and persuaded Prevost to make this a feature in his advertisements; he also secured permission for Blanche to practise in the ring every morning till her engagement began.

So he went back to the hotel elated, and explained to Blanche that, after all, in the theatrical life good management was half the battle. Now that she had shaken off that worthless Pelletier and he himself had taken charge of her affairs, she would undoubtedly be recognized in a very few years as the greatest acrobat in the world.

She must sit at once, in costume, for some new photographs, and he would send them to the leading managers of Europe and America. If they could only arrange to go to America under good auspices, their fortune would be made. Instead of receiving, as they were doing in Vienna, five hundred francs a week, they would be paid as much as twice that amount in New York, if not more. Indeed, Jules had so much to say about America, he seemed to have it on the brain.

Blanche experienced no difficulty in making her plunge in the new amphitheatre, and after her first trial there, declared that she had no fear for the public performances. Jules, however, insisted on her practising every morning; she must keep her muscles limber, he said; besides, if she didn't practise, she might lose confidence.

He found himself treating her as her mother had done, directing her movements like those of a child, and she obeyed him as if she considered his attitude toward her eminently natural and right. Even Madeleine adopted a motherly tone with her, chose the dresses she should wear each day, and instructed her in a thousand feminine details.

Blanche, Jules was surprised and secretly annoyed to discover, could speak German, and in the mornings she sometimes gave him lessons. He also picked up a good deal of German slang in the *cafés* that he frequented during the day, where he drank coffee and read whatever French and English papers he could find.

After his wife's performances began, he found himself falling into a routine of life. In spite of his distaste for his duties at the wool-house, he had expected to miss them at first; but he quickly became accustomed to his leisure. He really considered himself a busy person, for in addition to his nightly appearance in the arena, momentary but intensely dramatic, he spent considerable time in fraternizing with the Viennese journalists, to secure newspaper puffs for his wife, in conferring with Prevost, and in corresponding with managers for future engagements. After his first month in Vienna, he felt as if he had been connected with the circus for years.

Blanche heard constantly from home, from either her mother or one of the two girls,—more often from Louise than from Jeanne, who hated to write letters. Six weeks after her departure from Paris, her mother became Madame Berthier, without, as she had said, "any fuss," and was now installed with the children in the big house where Félix had passed so many lonely years as a bachelor. Jules and Blanche wrote a joint letter of congratulation, and after that Blanche seemed even happier than she had been; it was so good, she said, to think that the girls were provided for.

In the afternoons Jules took walks or drives with his wife, and on Sundays he accompanied her to early mass in the little church that they had discovered near their apartment. Blanche would have liked to go to high mass, but to this Jules strenuously objected; it was too long, and he couldn't understand the sermon, and altogether it made him sleepy. Sometimes on Sundays they would go to one of the *cafés* for *déjeuner* or dinner, and over this they used to be very happy, for it recalled the first months of their love.

After a time, however, these walks grew less frequent. Jules stayed at home more, and Madeleine became solicitous for Blanche's health. Jules had long talks with Prevost; Blanche had been engaged at the Circus for three months, and Prevost wished to reengage her for the spring season; but Jules explained that he had already received several offers for the spring, and had refused them all; his wife needed a long rest, and from Vienna they would go to Boulogne for a few months, to be with her people.

The reference to the engagements was not exactly true; Jules had one offer only for the summer; that was from Trouville. For the autumn he had a fairly generous offer from South America, and a better one from the Hippodrome in London, to begin on the first of December. He had practically decided to accept the offer from London; but before giving a definite answer, he resolved to consult Blanche about it.

"It will just fit in with our plans," he said. "On the first of May we'll take a good long rest. We'll go to your mother's old house. It hasn't been let yet, you know, and no one will want it before then. So you and Madeleine and I will live there together, and we'll pass the days out of doors, and take long walks by the sea, and forget all about the circus. Then, when you are well and strong again, we'll go to London, and astonish the English, who think there's nothing good in France. What do you say, dear? Don't you think that's a good plan?"

"Yes," she said slowly. "It will be very nice, Jules, if—"

"If? If what?"

"If I'm alive," she answered softly, turning her head away.

He took her in his arms and pressed his cheek against hers. "What a foolish little girl it is to talk like that! Of course you'll be alive, and you'll be even better and stronger and happier than you are now. And then think of all the good times you'll have this summer with Jeanne and Louise and your mother and Monsieur Berthier. We'll have *fêtes* for the girls at our house, and every day we'll go to see your mother. You don't think she'll be too proud to receive us, do you, now that she's rich and important? I suppose she's the queen of Boulogne, with her carriages and her horses and her servants. She'll soon be getting a husband for Jeanne, some fine young fellow with a lot of money. And won't Jeanne put him through his paces? She's a high-stepper, that Jeanne, and I should pity the man who got her and didn't understand her. Think of trying to keep Jeanne down!"

In her moments of depression he always spoke to her like that, and for the time it cheered her; but when the spring came, she drooped visibly, and Jules became alarmed; sometimes she would have attacks of convulsive weeping, and these would be followed by hours of profound sadness, during which she spoke scarcely a word. There were other days when she would be full of courage and hope, gayer than she had ever been; then they would drive into the country and she would take deep draughts of the fresh spring air, and her eyes would brighten and her cheeks flush.

In spite of his anxiety, these days were very happy for Jules; the thought that he might lose her made her dearer to him. Sometimes he would take her hand and tell her that without her he couldn't live; she had made him realize how wretched his existence had been before marriage; he could not go back to that again. Then she would rest her head on his shoulder and whisper that she would try to be brave. Her sufferings seemed to be wholly in her mind; the doctor Jules consulted said that, bodily, she was perfectly strong, and could easily fill her engagement at the circus; her work in the ring had given her a remarkable development of the muscles and the chest; if she stopped the work now, and ceased to practise, she would suffer from the inaction.

Jules, however, felt relieved when the fifteenth of April came, and they were able to leave Vienna for Paris. There they remained only a day, for they were eager to reach Boulogne and the little home that Madame Berthier had arranged for them, in the house where Blanche had been born, and had passed the few weeks in each year when she was not travelling.

When they arrived, early in the afternoon, Madame Berthier and the girls, together with Berthier, were at the station to meet them, and they received a rapturous greeting, the girls clinging to their sister with frantic embraces.

"We had *déjeuner* prepared for you at your house," said Madame, when the first greetings were over. "I knew you'd want to go there the first thing. Then to-night you are to come and dine with us. I feel as if I hadn't seen you for years."

"But we've never met Madame Berthier before," Jules replied, making a feeble attempt to be gay, for he saw that Blanche's meeting with her mother threatened to upset her.

Madame blushed like a young girl, and turning, led the way to the carriages.

"One of these is for you and Jules," she said. "I don't mean just for now, but for all the time you are here. Félix chose the horse for you, dear, and she's so gentle you can drive her alone if you want to."

"I'm going to put the three girls and their mother in the big carriage," Berthier said to Jules, "and you and Madeleine and I will follow them." The arrival of his stepdaughter seemed to have given him as much pleasure as any of the others, and his good-natured face was radiant. "Jump in, girls," he cried, holding out his hand to Blanche. "We'll have to turn those lilies of yours into roses this summer, my dear. Here, Jeanne, stop flirting with Jules, or we won't let you come with us. You wouldn't have known our little Louise, Blanche, if you hadn't expected to find her here, would you? She's grown an inch in four months. It's the most wonderful thing I've ever known in my life. And would you believe it?—she's become a perfect chatterbox—she's worse than Jeanne. Sometimes I have to run out of the room to read my paper in peace and have a quiet smoke."

The whole family seemed to have agreed to assume toward Blanche the bantering tone that Jules had adopted. When they reached the house they continued their gayety, though Blanche, tired from her journey, sank weakly on the couch in the *salon*.

She looked around, however, and saw that the room had been redecorated, probably by Monsieur Berthier, and when she felt rested she went all over the house and observed many new pieces of furniture, and many touches here and there that made the place more attractive and homelike. "Ah, it is so good to be at home," she said to her mother when they were alone; and then Madame Berthier took her in her arms and kissed her on the forehead and told her she must have courage for Jules' sake.

After the excitement of Paris and Vienna, Jules found it hard to accustom himself to the dull life at Boulogne. He bought a small yacht, and found amusement in sailing with his new acquaintances, and sometimes, when the weather was fine, he took Blanche and the girls with him. He also occupied himself with the little garden around his cottage; but this soon bored him, and he gave it over to Monsieur Berthier's gardener, who came every few days to look after it. In the afternoons he drove with Blanche far into the country, and sometimes they stopped at a little *café* by the roadside and had an early dinner, and then hurried home before the damp night should close around them.

On these occasions they had many earnest talks, and Jules was surprised by the seriousness and depth of his wife's mind; at any rate, she impressed him as being wonderfully profound. The longer he knew her, the more she awed and puzzled him; there were moments when she seemed to dwell in another world, a world that made her almost a stranger to him.

Since her return to Boulogne she had grown much more cheerful than she had been during those last weeks in Vienna; but a thousand little things she said showed him that beneath the surface of her thought there still lurked a strange melancholy, an unchangeable conviction that life was slipping away from her. He spoke of this once to her mother, and she explained mysteriously that he must expect that; it was very natural with one of Blanche's temperament. She had known many cases like it before.

As the summer passed, Jules said little to his wife about the circus; indeed, her work was scarcely mentioned between them, though every morning she practised her exercises. Jules, however, had decided that they should go to London late in November and, the first week of the following month, appear at the Hippodrome, which had been established with great success the year before, at a short distance from the Houses of Parliament. The contract had not been signed, for Jules had written to Marshall, the manager, that he could not bind himself to an engagement until early in the autumn; but he explained that his word was as good as any contract.

When September came, Blanche seemed much better for her months of rest; her eyes were brighter, and her cheeks were shot with color. Sometimes Jules wished that she were not quite so religious; she went to early mass every morning now, and rather than let her go alone, he went with her, for Madeleine had assumed the duties of the household. Their evenings, which during the summer had been spent chiefly on the porch of Monsieur Berthier's house, were now passed in their *salon*, bright with flowers, sometimes with a wood-fire crackling on the old-fashioned hearth. Blanche's fingers were always busy with soft, fleecy garments, which Jules used sometimes to take in his hands and rub affectionately against his face. Then he often noticed a light in her eyes that he had never seen before; it reminded him of pictures of the Madonna. Sometimes he was so touched when he looked at her that he would take her in his arms and hold her close for a long while. Their evenings together became very dear to him; yet they said little to each other: he was content to sit and watch her, with the curtains drawn to shut out the rest of the world.

Occasionally Father Duményy would come in for an hour's chat. He was a large-framed, heavy man, with deep gray eyes shaded by enormous eyebrows that moved up and down as he spoke. He spoke as he walked, slowly and lumberingly, and he had a quaint humor that used to delight Blanche and puzzle Jules. When he appeared, she always brightened, and she liked to hear his doleful accounts of his rheumatism. He seemed to find humor in everything, even in his arduous duties and his ailments.

"Ah, my children," he would say, "why should any one go to the theatre for pleasure? This life is nothing but a comedy, if you only look at it in the right way."

From Blanche he derived a great deal of amusement; that she should perform in a circus always seemed a joke to him, and he was continually making fun over it. He had never been at a circus; so, though he had baptized Blanche and had met her during her visits in Boulogne, he had never seen her perform. Once when Jules showed him a photograph of Blanche as she appeared while posing on the rope, he rolled his eyes and pretended to be much shocked, and they all laughed together.

"I suppose you two people will be leaving this nest of yours before winter comes," he said one night. "You've made your plans already, haven't you?"

Jules looked down at Blanche, but she avoided his eyes.

"We haven't decided definitely," Jules replied, "but we think of going to London."

Blanche sighed, and Father Dumény glanced at her quickly and then smiled up at Jules.

"She has a notion that she isn't going to live," Jules added, nodding at his wife. "Ridiculous, isn't it?"

Father Duményy put his hands to his sides, and for a moment his great body shook with laughter.

"Why, I expect to baptize at least half a dozen of your children! In a few years we shall see them trotting around here in Boulogne and coming to my Sunday-school to be prepared for their first communion. We need all the good Catholics we can have, in these days, to fight against the infidelity that's ruining the country. Ah, my dear child," he said, patting Blanche's hand, "when you're a grandmother with a troop of children around you, you'll look back and smile at these foolish little fears."

After that night he came oftener, and kept Blanche laughing with his gayety.

"When you go to London," he said one evening, "I shall give you letters to some dear English friends of mine,—Mr. and Mrs. Tate. I met the Tates when I was in Paris visiting Father Brémont more than ten years ago. Mr. Tate represented the banking-house of Welling Brothers, of London, there, and now he's in London as a member of the firm, I believe. You'll like Mrs. Tate, my dear. She's a good soul, and she speaks French almost as well as English. I shall expect to hear that you've become great friends."

"But we aren't sure of going to England yet," Blanche replied with a weary smile.

"Perhaps we shall go to America," Jules laughed. "I want Blanche to see the country."

Toward the end of September Blanche drooped again, and her mother was with her nearly every moment of the day, remaining sometimes till late at night. The girls had gone back to the convent, but they were allowed to come home twice a week, and most of their freedom they devoted to their sister, whom they treated with a protecting tenderness that used to afford Jules secret amusement. Madame Berthier maintained a cheerful composure in her daughter's presence, but when alone with Jules she became so serious that for the first time he grew nervous. Then as his anxiety deepened he began to resent it, as he did any long-continued annoyance. Why should they be kept in idleness and suspense so long? How stupid to be buried in a wretched provincial town when they might be earning thousands of francs in Vienna, or Bucharest, or Paris!

Then one night he was suddenly aroused from his sleep, and he felt a sensation of mingled horror and awe. He dressed himself quickly, his whole being wrung by the groans he heard from the next room, and tore out of the house to Doctor Brutinière's, five minutes away. After delivering his message, he ran breathlessly to summon Madame Berthier. It took her scarcely five minutes to dress, and then they were in the street together. Madame Berthier went at once to Blanche's room, and Jules paced up and down in the half-lighted *salon*.

That was the ghastliest night of Jules Le Baron's life. He was overwhelmed by the knowledge that Blanche was in agony, that she was battling for life, that at any moment he might hear she was dead. Why should the burden of suffering fall on her? Oh, how cruel Nature was, how pitiless to women! The poor child, the poor little one, to be tortured so! Several times he listened for a sound, and the silence terrified him. Suddenly he heard a shriek, loud and piercing, that only the most exquisite pain could have wrung, and he clenched his hands in impotent horror and misery.

The stillness that followed made him fear that she was dead, and he could hardly keep from rushing up the stairs and learning the truth. After a few moments, as he stood at the door, he heard another cry, small, timorous, peevish, that changed to a wail and then died away. He turned into the room, clapsed his face in his hands, and cried, "Thank God, thank God! And mercy for her, my God, mercy for my poor little Blanche!"

After what seemed to him a long time, during which he was tortured with suspense, a door opened and shut, and he heard a rustling on the stairs. He stepped out into the hall and saw Madame Berthier descending. She stopped, smiled, and put her hand to her lips; he could see traces of tears in her eyes.

"Come up," she whispered. "It's all over. It's a girl, and Blanche has her in her arms."

Jules bounded up the stairs. "Only a minute, you know," she said softly, "and you must be very quiet."

When she opened the door he almost pushed her aside in his eagerness to enter. The Doctor and Madeleine were standing beside the bed, where Blanche, white but bright-eyed and smiling, was lying with the babe nestling close to her. Jules flung himself by her side, and kissed her passionately, murmuring incoherent words of love and thankfulness.

Chapter XII

The weeks of convalescence that followed were the happiest Blanche had ever known. She felt wrapped in the devotion of her husband and her family, and exalted by her love for her child. At moments she feared that she could not live through such happiness. Sometimes she would fancy that all her sufferings had been only a dream, and then she would turn and find with a thrill of joy the babe lying beside her. Jules would sit by the bed holding her hand, and making jokes about their daughter's future. They had decided that she should be called Jeanne, and no one but Father Dumény should baptize her.

One morning, when Blanche was sitting up in bed for the first time, Jules entered the room with a letter in his hand and in his face a look of exultation.

"It's from Marshall," he said, "from the Hippodrome in London, you know. He wants me to make a contract for six months, from the first of January. I was afraid he might back out because we held off so long. But this makes it all right. You'll have more than a month to get strong again and to practise in."

Jules was so excited by the prospect that he did not notice the look of alarm that had appeared in his wife's eyes. She lay still, with one arm extended on the coverlet, her head leaning to one side, and her dark hair making a background for her white face.

"'We want you to open on the first,'" Jules read aloud. "'Let us hear from you as soon as possible and we will send on the contract for your signature.' Of course," he went on, folding the note, "we must jump at it. What do you say?"

For a moment she looked at him without speaking. Then she replied weakly, "Do what you think best, Jules."

"Good!" he said, jumping up. "I'll write now. We've lost a lot of time, you know, and we must make up for it when we get back to work."

"Do you—do you think I'll be strong enough?" she went on, as if she hadn't heard him.

"Strong enough!" he laughed. "Of course you'll be strong enough in seven weeks more. You're nearly your old self now," he added affectionately. "Don't you worry about that."

When he had closed the door and left her alone, she felt as if her body were sinking into the bed from weakness. The circus again! That ghastly plunge! Since the birth of her child she had hardly thought of it. Now the thought horrified her! How could she leave her babe and risk her life night after night? Perhaps some night—oh! it was too horrible. She couldn't, she couldn't! She lifted her hands to her face as if to shut out the horror of the thought. Then she turned to the little Jeanne who was sleeping beside her, and drew her close to her bosom.

She had lost courage! It would never come back to her. When Jules returned she would tell him, and she would beg him, for Jeanne's sake, to give up that engagement in London till she felt well again. Oh, if they could only leave the circus forever! If she could only do as other women did, devote her life to her child. The circus was no place for a mother.

Then it suddenly flashed upon her that if she said these things to Jules he would urge her to place Jeanne in her mother's care while they were in England; but to that she would never consent, never. She would rather give up performing altogether. Yes, when Jules came back she would speak of this. He loved the circus, but for Jeanne's sake he would give it up, she knew he would.

But when Jules did return, he was so enthusiastic about the engagement in London that she did not dare oppose it. "Think of the sensation we'll make there!" he said. "How those stupid English will open their eyes! And then we'll surely have big offers from other places. After a London success we can make a fortune in America. They say the Americans are crazy over everything that makes a hit in London. Oh," he went on, stretching his arms and yawning, "it will be a relief to get out of this dull old town. Think of the months we've wasted here. I feel rusty already."

Something in his tone as well as his words frightened her, and a feeling of helplessness came over her when he put his hand on her forehead and said gently: "You must try to get strong as soon as possible, dear. Think of all the practising you'll have to do for your plunge."

She turned her head away, and he observed nothing strange in her manner. She wanted to speak of taking Jeanne with them, but a fear that he might object restrained her.

Two days later, when her mother and Jules were in the room together, Madame Berthier, with apparent carelessness, asked what they were going to do with the little one while they were travelling. "Of course you can't carry her about with you. So you'd better leave her with me. I'll take the best of care of her."

She was startled by the light that flashed into her daughter's eyes. "No, no!" Blanche cried. "We shall keep her with us always. I couldn't bear to leave her here. I couldn't—I couldn't go away without her."

Madame Berthier and Jules exchanged glances, and Blanche saw that her intuition was correct. They had been discussing the project of leaving the child in Boulogne. She felt as if they were conspiring against her.

"Don't you think it would be better if your mother—" Jules began, but Blanche cut him short.

"We shall have Madeleine. She will help me to take care of Jeanne. I couldn't go without her," she repeated, with tears in her voice.

"There, there!" said Madame Berthier, becoming alarmed. "Have your own way. Perhaps it's better that you should keep the child with you."

Blanche read annoyance in her husband's face, but she said nothing. A few moments later, Madame Berthier left the room and Jules followed. She knew they had gone to discuss the little scene that had just taken place. But she resolved that she would not give up the child! Rather than do that she would stay in Boulogne.

The fear of being separated from Jeanne, made her decide not to refer in any way to her terror of the plunge. That might strengthen Jules' belief that the presence of the child disturbed her, and he might insist on a separation. Besides, she tried to convince herself that as she grew stronger her nervousness would disappear. It must of course be due solely to her weak condition. Once restored to health, the plunge would be, as it always had been, merely part of her daily routine.

But in spite of her rapidly increasing strength, Blanche found that after three weeks she was still depressed by the thought of her season in London. Jules complained that she was devoting herself too much to Jeanne; she must drive out more, and walk with the girls, and give more time to her exercises. Her mother, too, grew severe with her. "One would think there never was another child in the world," she said, and then Blanche suspected that Jules had been complaining of her. "The little one is a dear, and I love her," Madame Berthier continued, "but you have your work to do, and you must think of that too. No wonder Jules is growing impatient."

Jules had already received the contract for the engagement at the Hippodrome, and on signing it at his request, Blanche had had a horrible fancy that she was putting her signature to a warrant for her own doom. Once she thought of confiding her fear to her mother, but her mother would be sure to repeat what she said to Jules. At any cost, she felt she must hide it from him. Then she determined to tell Father Duményy, but when the moment came she had not courage to put her feeling into words, and she was ashamed of it as a superstition. So she decided that she would keep the miserable secret to herself, finding no relief save in gusts of weeping when she was alone with the child.

Once Jules found her with traces of tears in her eyes. "What's the matter?" he asked gently, taking her hand.

She turned her head away. "I don't feel well," she said.

He looked at her closely. "You'll be well when you get back to your work. That's what the matter is. You aren't used to being idle. The best thing for us to do is to leave here the day after Christmas. That will give you nearly a week for practice in London, and we'll have time to look about for rooms there. Since we are going to have Jeanne with us, we'll want to take an apartment in some quiet street."

When he went away she sat for a long time without speaking. In a week they would be far away from this place, among strangers. She wondered why she had not suffered so on leaving home before. Until now she had regarded the circus as part of her life; she had not hoped for any other kind of life. How strange it was that Jules should love it so! Sometimes it seemed— —But it was right that she should go on with her work, for she must earn money for the little Jeanne now. Perhaps in a few years she would make a fortune, and then Jules could not object to her leaving the circus. But before a few years passed she would be obliged to go through her performance more than a thousand times. At this thought her heart seemed to stop beating, and then it thumped against her side.

Their Christmas in Boulogne at Monsieur Berthier's house reminded them of their *fête* in Paris of the year before. Berthier himself led in the gayety, and the girls were in the wildest spirits. Blanche sat among them with the child in her arms, looking, as Jules said, as if she were posing for a Madonna. In the evening Father Dumény came to bid his friends good-bye. He pretended to pinch the little Jeanne on the cheek, and he made jokes with Blanche about her terror before the child's birth. "She's the healthiest baby I've ever baptized," he said. "You should have heard her roar when I poured the water on her head. That's a good sign. I suppose you'll make a great performer of her too," he continued, smiling into the face of the mother, but growing serious when he saw the effect of the question.

"Never!" exclaimed Blanche.

"We're going to earn a fortune for her," said Jules with a smile. "So she won't have to work at all. We'll settle down in Paris and make a fine lady of her, and marry her into the nobility."

Blanche did not speak again for a long time. They knew she was depressed at the thought of leaving home the next day. When Father Dumény rose, he took a letter from the pocket of his long black coat.

"I almost forgot about this. Here's the introduction I promised you to my friends in London. You will like Mrs. Tate, my dear," he said to Blanche, "and she'll make a great pet of the little one. She hasn't any children of her own, poor woman. Be sure to go to see them," he concluded, "and present my compliments to them."

When he was gone, Jules shrugged his shoulders and turned to his wife. "What do we want to meet those people for?" he said. "What will they care about us?"

The next day they left Boulogne, after many farewell injunctions from the Berthiers, and much weeping on the part of Blanche and her sisters. Blanche stood for a long time with Madeleine, who held the little Jeanne in her arms, waving farewell to her kindred on the wharf, and watching the shores of France recede from her gaze. When the last vestige of land disappeared in the wintry fog and she found herself shut in by the shoreless sea, she turned away with a feeling of hopeless weariness. She had a morbid presentiment that she was leaving home forever.

Chapter XIII

Mrs. Tate ran her eyes over the pile of letters at her plate on the breakfast-table. She was a large, florid woman of forty, verging on stoutness, with an abundance of reddish-brown hair.

"What a lot of mail!" she said to her husband, who was absorbed in reading the "Daily Telegraph,"—a small man, with black hair and moustache tinged with gray, and small black eyes finely wrinkled at the corners. "Here's a letter from Amy dated at Cannes. They must have left Paris sooner than they intended; and here's something from Fanny Mayo,—an invitation to dinner, I suppose. Fanny told me she wanted us to meet the Presbreys next week,—some people she knew in Bournemouth."

"Fanny's always taking up new people," said Tate from behind his paper, "and dropping them in a month."

"And here's something else with a French stamp on it. Let me see. From Boulogne? It must be from Father Dumény. Yes, I recognize the handwriting."

"Another subscription, I suppose," her husband grunted.

"He hasn't written for nearly a year. I wonder what started him this time. What a dear old soul he is! Do you remember the night we took him out to a restaurant in Paris and he was so afraid of being seen? I always laugh when I think of that."

"What's he got to say?"

With her knife, Mrs. Tate cut one end of the letter open, and her eye wandered slowly down the page.

"He's been ill, he says, but he's able to be about now. He came near running over here last summer, but he couldn't get away." For a few moments Mrs. Tate was absorbed in reading; then she exclaimed with a curious little laugh: "How funny! Listen to this, will you? He's left what he really wrote for till the end,—like a woman. He wants us to look after a *protégée* of his, a girl that he baptized, the daughter of an acrobat. Did you ever hear of such a thing? She's in the circus herself, and she's going to appear at the Hippodrome next week. She performs on the trapeze, and then she dives backward from the roof of the building—backward, mind you! Could anything be more terrible?"

"I should think she'd be right in your line," Tate replied without lifting his eyes from his paper. "She'll be something new. You can make a lion of her."

"Don't be impertinent, Percy. This is a very serious matter. It seems the girl's married and had a child about two months ago. She's going to resume her performances. She doesn't know a soul in London; so she'll be all alone."

"I thought you said she had a husband."

"So I did. He's given them a letter to us, but he doesn't think they'll present it. I suppose those theatrical people live in a world of their own. But of course I shall go to see her. Perhaps I can do something for her. Anyway, it'll be interesting to meet an acrobat. I've never known one in my life."

"As I said," her husband remarked, turning to his bacon and eggs, "you can introduce her into society. People must be tired of meeting artists and actors and musicians. She'll be a novelty."

"You're very disagreeable to-day, Percy," Mrs. Tate responded amiably, after sipping the coffee that had been steaming beside her plate. "You are always attributing the meanest motives to everything I do."

He gave a short laugh. "But you must acknowledge that you do some pretty queer things, my dear."

She ignored the remark, and a moment later she went on briskly: "I must go and see this acrobat woman—whoever she is. If I don't—"

"What's her name?" Tate asked, turning to his paper and searching for the theatrical columns.

"Madame Jules Le Baron, Father Dumény calls her. But I suppose she must have a stage name. Most of them have."

"I don't see that name in 'Under the Clock!' The Hippodrome? No, it isn't there. I wonder if this can be the one: 'On Monday evening next, Mademoiselle Blanche, the celebrated French acrobat, will give her remarkable performance on the trapeze and her great dive from the top of the Hippodrome.'"

Mrs. Tate sighed.

"Yes, it must be. Mademoiselle Blanche! How stagey it sounds! I wonder what she's like."

"We might go to see her first and then we could tell whether she's possible or not."

"Go to the Hippodrome!"

"Yes, why not? It's perfectly respectable. Only it doesn't happen to be fashionable. In Paris, you know, it's the thing to attend the circus. Don't you remember the La Marches took us one night?"

"Yes, and I remember there was a dreadful creature—she must have weighed three hundred pounds—who walked the tight-rope and nearly frightened me to death. I thought she'd come down on my head."

"Then it's understood that we're to go on Monday? If we go at all we might as well be there the first night. It'll be more interesting."

Mrs. Percy Tate was a personage in London. For several years before her marriage, at the age of twenty-five, she had been known as an heiress and a belle. Even then she had a reputation for independence of character, and for an indefatigable zeal for reforming the world. Her name stood at the head of several charitable societies, and she was also a member of many clubs for the improvement of the physical and spiritual condition of the human race. Since her marriage she had grown somewhat milder; her friends used to say that Percy Tate had "trained" her. They also said that she had "made" him; without her money he would never have become a member of the rich firm of Welling and Company.

Percy Tate's business associates, however, knew the fallacy of this uncharitable opinion. With his dogged determination and his keen insight into the intricacies of finance, Tate was sure of forging ahead in time, with or without backing. His association with Welling and Company gave the house even greater strength than it had had before; for in addition to his reputation as a financier, he had made his name a synonym for stanch integrity. He had passed sixteen happy years with his wife, wisely directed her charities, wholesomely ridiculed her enthusiasms, followed her into the Catholic Church, where he was quite as sincere if a much less ardent worshipper; and in all the serious things of life he treated her, not as an inferior to be patronized, but as an equal that he respected, with no display of sentiment, but with sincere devotion. She, on her part, was amused by his humor and guided by his advice, though she often pretended to ignore it; and she never allowed any of her numerous undertakings to interfere with her regard for his comfort or the happiness of her home.

The manager of the Hippodrome had extensively advertised the appearance of Mademoiselle Blanche, and on Monday night the amphitheatre was crowded. The Tates arrived early in order to see the whole performance; as they had never been at the Hippodrome before, the evening promised to be amusing for them. Tate, however, became so interested in the menagerie through which they passed before entering the portion of the vast building devoted to the exhibitions in the ring that they remained there more than an hour. The interval between their taking seats and the appearance of the acrobat rather bored them.

"I wish they'd hurry up and let her come out," said Mrs. Tate. "And yet I almost dread seeing her make that horrible plunge. This must be the first time she's done it since the birth of her baby. Isn't it really shocking?"

"Oh, I suppose these people are as much entitled to babies as any other people."

She cast a reproachful glance at him, and did not reply for a moment. Then she said: "But what must her feelings be now—just as she's getting ready?"

"I dare say she's glad to get back to her work and earn her salary again. Her husband probably doesn't earn anything. Those fellows never do."

"She must be frightened nearly to death."

Tate laughed softly. "You'll die from worrying about other people."

"What are they doing now?" Mrs. Tate asked, turning her eyes to the ring. "I suppose that rope they're letting down is for her to climb up on, and that's the net she'll fall into. How gracefully that trapeze swings! I feel quite excited. Every one else is too. Can't you see it in their faces? There must be thousands of people here. How strange they look! Such coarse faces."

"It's the great British middle class. This is just the kind of thing they like."

"It reminds me of pictures of the Colosseum. I can almost fancy their turning their thumbs down. Here she comes. How light she is on her feet! And isn't she pretty! But she looks awfully thin and delicate, and she's as pale as a ghost."

"You'll attract all the people round us. Of course she's pale. She's probably powdered up to the eyes, like the women we used to see in Paris."

"How lightly she goes up that rope," Mrs. Tate whispered, "and what wonderful arms she has! Just like a man's. They look as if they didn't belong to her body."

Silently and dexterously Blanche reached the main trapeze, and for a moment she sat there, with her arms crooked against the rope on either side and rubbing her hands. For the first time during her career she was terrified in the ring. She had hoped that as soon as she resumed her work the terror she had felt since Jeanne's birth would pass away. Now, however, it made her so weak that she feared she was going to fall.

She was thinking of the child as she had seen her crowing in the crib. If anything should happen to her she might never see Jeanne again. She was vaguely conscious of the vast mass of people below her, waiting for her to move. She took a long breath and nerved herself for the start, before making her spring to the trapeze below; she must have courage for the sake of the little Jeanne, she said to herself. Mechanically she began to sway forward and backward; then she shot into the air, and with a sensation of surprise and delight she continued her performance.

Mrs. Tate watched her with an expression of mingled fear, interest, and pleasure in her face.

"Isn't she the most wonderful creature you ever saw, Percy?" she cried, clutching her husband's arm. "It's horrible, yet I can't help looking. Suppose she should fall!"

"She'd merely drop into the net. There's nothing very dangerous about what she's doing now. Keep still."

"I never saw anything more graceful. She *is* grace itself, isn't she? See how her hair flies; I should think it would get into her eyes and blind her. I shall speak to her about that when I see her. I shall certainly *go* to see her."

In a round of applause, Blanche finished her performance on the trapeze and then began her posing on the rope, whirling slowly, with a rhythmic succession of motions to the net. Then Jules, in evening dress, with a large diamond gleaming in his shirt-front, stepped out on the net, and for an instant they conferred together. Suddenly she clapped her hands, bounded on the rope again, and while Jules held it to steady her motion, she climbed hand over hand to the top of the building. There she sat, looking in the distance like a white bird ready to take flight, her dark hair streaming around her head.

"I feel as if I were going to faint," Mrs. Tate whispered.

Her husband glanced at her quickly. "Yes, you'd better—in this crowd. A fine panic you'd create! Want to go out?"

She seemed to pull herself together. "No, I think I shall be able to bear it. If I can't, I'll look away. What's that he's saying? What horrible English he speaks! I can't understand a word. *Oh!*" she gasped, clutching her husband by one arm and holding him firmly as Blanche dropped backward and whirled through the air; and this exclamation she repeated in a tone of horrified relief when the girl struck the net, bounded into the air again, and landed on her feet.

They rose with the applauding crowd and started to leave the place. "In my opinion," said Mrs. Tate, clinging to her husband's arm and drawing her wrap closely around her, "in my opinion such exhibitions are outrageous. There ought to be a law against them. Think of that poor little creature going through that every night. Of course she'll be killed sometime. I wonder if she's afraid. I should think she'd expect every night to be her last."

"What nonsense you're talking. Of course those people don't feel like that. If they did they'd never go into the business. It's second nature to them."

"But they're *human* just like the rest of us, and that woman is a mother," Mrs. Tate insisted. "Don't you suppose she thinks of her baby before she makes that terrible dive? It's a shame that her husband should allow her to do it."

"There you are, trying to regulate the affairs of the world again. Why don't you let people alone? They'd be a good deal happier, and so would you. Her husband probably likes to have her do it."

"Well, I shall go to see her anyway," Mrs. Tate cried with determination. "Then I can find out all about her for myself."

For the next three weeks Mrs. Tate was absorbed by various duties in connection with her charitable societies. One morning, however, she suddenly realized that she had neglected to comply with Father Dumény's request, and she resolved to put off her other engagements for the afternoon and call at once on the acrobat; if she didn't go then, there was no knowing when she could go. At four o'clock she found herself stepping into a hansom in front of her house in Cavendish Square.

The address that Father Dumény had sent led her to a little French hotel with a narrow, dark entrance, dimly lighted by an odorous lamp. She poked about in the place for a moment, wondering how she was to find any one; then a door which she had not observed was thrown open, and she was confronted by a little man with a very waxed moustache, who smiled and asked in broken English what Madame wanted. She stammered that she was looking for Madame Le Baron, and the little man at once called a *garçon* in a greasy apron, who led the way up the narrow stairs. When they had reached the second landing the boy rapped on the door, and Mrs. Tate stood panting behind him. For several moments there was no answer; then heavy steps could be heard approaching, and a moment later Madeleine's broad figure, silhouetted by the light from the windows from behind, stood before them. Mrs. Tate saw at a glance that she was French, and addressed her in her own language.

"*Mais oui*," Madeleine replied. "Madame is at home. Will Madame have the goodness to enter?"

"Say that I'm Father Dumény's friend, please," said Mrs. Tate as she gave Madeleine a card. Then she glanced at one corner of the room, where a large cradle, covered with a lace canopy, had caught her eye. "Is the baby here?" she asked quickly, going toward it.

"Ah, no—not now. She sometimes sleeps here in the morning; but she is with her mother in the other room now."

Madeleine disappeared, and Mrs. Tate's eyes roved around the room. She recognized it at once as the typical English lodging-house drawing-room; she had seen many rooms just like it before, when she had called on American friends living for a time in London. It was large and oblong, facing the tall houses on the opposite side of the street that cut off much of the light; the wall paper was ugly and sombre, and the carpet, with its large flowery pattern, together with the lounge and chairs, completed an effect of utter dreariness.

Mrs. Tate wondered how people could live in such places; she should simply go mad if she had to stay in a room like this. Then she wondered why Madame Le Baron hadn't brightened up the apartment a bit; the photographs on the mantel, in front of the large French mirror, together with the cradle in the corner, were the only signs it gave of being really inhabited. How vulgar those prints on the wall were! They and the mirror were the only French touches visible, and they contrasted oddly with their surroundings. While Mrs. Tate was comfortably meditating on the vast superiority of England to France, the door leading to the next room opened and Blanche entered the room. She looked so domestic in her simple dress of blue serge that for an instant her caller did not recognize her.

She held out her hand timidly. "Father Dumény has spoken to me about you," she said.

"Father Dumény must think I am an extremely rude person. I meant to come weeks ago," Mrs. Tate replied, clasping the hand and looking down steadily into the pale face. "But I've been busy—so busy, I've had hardly a minute to myself. However, I did go to see you perform."

"Ah, at the Hippodrome?"

"Yes, the very first night. Mr. Tate and I went together. We were both—er—wonderfully impressed. I don't think I ever saw anything more wonderful in my life than that plunge of yours."

Mrs. Tate adjusted herself in the chair near the window, and Blanche took the opposite seat. "I'm glad you liked it," she said with a sigh.

"Liked it. I can't really say I did like it. I must confess it rather horrified me."

"It does some people. My mother never likes to see me do it—though I've done it for a great many years now."

"But doesn't it—doesn't it make you nervous sometimes?"

"I never used to think of it—before my baby was born."

"Ah, the baby! May I see her? Just a peep."

"She was asleep when I left," Blanche replied, unconsciously lowering her voice as if the child in the next room might know she was being talked about; "but she will wake up soon. She always wakes about this time. Madeleine is with her now, and she'll dress her and bring her in."

For a quarter of an hour they talked about the little Jeanne, and Blanche, inspired by Mrs. Tate's vivid interest and sympathy, grew animated in describing the baby's qualities; when she was born she weighed nearly nine pounds, and she had not been sick a day. Then she had grown so! You could hardly believe it was the same child. She very rarely cried,—almost never at night. Mrs. Tate had heard mothers talk like that before, but Blanche's *naïveté* lent a new charm to the narration; she kept in mind, however, their first topic, and at the next opportunity she returned to it.

"Then what do you do with the child at night?" she asked. "I suppose your servant goes to the circus with you, doesn't she? Of course you can't leave the baby alone."

"Ah, no," Blanche replied. "We have a little girl to stay with her."

Mrs. Tate was surprised. So these circus people lived as other people did, with servants to wait on them, with a nurse for the child. She had instinctively thought of them as vagabonds. On discovering that they were well cared for, she had a sensation very like disappointment; they seemed to be in no need of help of any sort. She was curious to know more of the life of this girl, who seemed so *naïve* and had such a curious look of sadness in her eyes. Mrs. Tate deftly led Blanche to talk about her husband, and in a few minutes, by her questions and her quick intelligence, she fancied that she understood the condition of this extraordinary *ménage*.

Percy had been right; the wife supported the family and the husband was a mere hanger-on; but it was evident from the way he was mentioned that the romance still lasted. Then Blanche made a reference to Jules which led her visitor to make inquiries with regard to him, and these changed her view of the situation. So, before marriage, Monsieur had been in business, and he had probably given it up to follow his wife in her wanderings. She surmised that they were not absolutely dependent on the circus for their daily bread; perhaps this accounted for their comfortable way of living.

While apparently absorbed in conversation Mrs. Tate continued this train of thought. She had never known any one connected with the circus before, she explained with a smile; people who lived in London all the time were apt to be so very narrow and ignorant; but she wanted to hear all about it, and Madame must tell her. Blanche was able to tell very little, for she was not used to discussing her work. By adroit questioning, however, Mrs. Tate led her on to an account of her early career from her first appearance as a child with her father to her development into a "star" performer.

The narrative seemed to her wildly interesting. How fascinating it would be if she could persuade the girl to relate her story in a drawing-room! It would be the sensation of the winter. But this poor child never could talk in public, even in her own tongue.

"But do tell me," said Mrs. Tate, when Blanche had described the months her father had spent in teaching her to make the great plunge. "Doesn't it hurt your back? I should think that striking with full force day after day on that padded net would destroy the nervous system of a giant."

Blanche smiled and shook her head. "It never used to hurt. I've only felt it lately, since the baby was born," she said.

"Then it does hurt now?" Mrs. Tate cried eagerly.

"Sometimes. I feel so tired in the morning now. I never used to; and sometimes when I wake up my back aches very much. But I try not to think of it."

"But, my dear child, you ought to think of it. You mustn't allow yourself to be injured—perhaps for life."

Blanche turned pale. "Do you think it can be serious?" she asked timidly.

Mrs. Tate saw that she had made a false step. "Of course not—not *serious*. It's probably nothing at all. I haven't a doubt a physician could stop it easily. Have you spoken to any one about it?"

"No; not even to my husband. I shouldn't like to tell him. It would make him unhappy."

Mrs. Tate became thoughtful. "I wonder if Dr. Broughton couldn't do something for you. He's our physician, and he's the kindest soul in the world. I'm always sending him to people. Suppose I should ask him to come and call on you some day. Perhaps he'll tell you there's nothing the matter, and then you won't be worried any more." She glanced into the pale face and was startled by the look she saw there. "Oh, you needn't be afraid," she laughed. "He won't hurt you. But, of course, if you don't want him to come, I won't send him."

Blanche clasped her hands and dropped her eyes. "I think I should like to have him come if—if—my husband— —"

"But he needn't know anything about it," said Mrs. Tate, with feminine delight at the prospect of secrecy. "We won't tell him anything. If he meets Monsieur Le Baron here you can just say I sent him to call on you. Besides, he can come some time when your husband isn't here," she added with a smile.

"Jules generally goes out in the afternoon," Blanche replied, feeling guilty at the thought of concealing anything from him. "He likes to read the French papers in a *café* in the Strand."

"Then I'll tell Dr. Broughton to come some afternoon. He'll be delighted. I don't believe *he's* ever known an acrobat either," she laughed.

They talked more of Blanche's symptoms, and Mrs. Tate speedily discovered that since the birth of the baby Blanche had not been free from terror of her work; every night she feared might be her last. She did not confess this directly, but Mrs. Tate gathered it from several intimations and from her own observations. She felt elated. What an interesting case! She had never heard of anything like it before. This poor child was haunted with a horrible terror! This accounted for the pitiful look of distress in her eyes. Then Mrs. Tate's generous heart fairly yearned with sympathy; but this she was careful to conceal. She saw that by displaying it she would do far more harm than good; so she pretended to be amused at the possibility of Blanche's injuring herself in making the plunge.

"It must have become second nature to you," she said, "after all these years. You're probably a little tired and nervous. Dr. Broughton will give you a tonic that will restore your old confidence. Meantime," she added enthusiastically, "I'm going to take care of you. I'm coming to see you very often, and I shall expect you to come to see me. Let me think; this is Thursday. On Sunday night you and Monsieur Le Baron must come and dine with us at seven o'clock. We'll be all alone. I sha'n't ask any one. But wait a minute. Why wouldn't that be a good way for your husband to meet Dr. Broughton? I'll ask him to come, too. He often looks in on Sundays. That will be delightful."

She rose to her feet and shook out her skirts. "I suppose I must go without seeing the baby. But I shall——" She looked quickly around at the clicking sound that seemed to come from the door. Then the door opened, and Jules, in a heavy fur-trimmed coat and silk hat, stood before her. She recognized him at once, and as he bowed hesitatingly, she extended her hand and relieved the awkwardness of the situation. "I won't wait for Madame to introduce me," she said, just as Blanche was murmuring her name.

"Then you are the lady Father Dumény spoke to us about!" Jules said with a smile.

"Yes; and your wife and I have become the best of friends already."

"And you've made friends with the baby too, I hope," Jules replied, removing his coat and throwing it over a chair. She liked his face more than she had done at the Hippodrome; he had a good eye, and, for a Frenchman, a remarkably clear complexion.

"No; she's asleep," Blanche replied. "I asked Madeleine to bring her in if she woke up."

"But you must see her," Jules insisted. "I'll go and take a peep at her."

He went to the door leading to the next room, opened it softly, and glanced in. Then he made a sign that the others were to follow, and he tiptoed toward the bed where Jeanne lay sleeping, her face rosy with health, and her little hands tightly closed. Madeleine, who had been sitting beside the bed, rose as they approached and showed her mouthful of teeth.

For a few moments they stood around the child, smiling at one another and without speaking. Then they tiptoed out of the room, and closed the door behind them.

"I shall come again soon some morning," Mrs. Tate whispered, as if still afraid of disturbing the child, "when the baby's awake." Then she went on in a louder tone: "She's a dear. I know I shall become very fond of her. And you're coming to us next Sunday night," she added, as she bade Jules good-bye. "Your wife has promised. I shall expect you both. Perhaps I shall come before then; I want to get acquainted with Jeanne."

She kissed Blanche on both cheeks, after the French fashion. "I sha'n't forget, you know. We have great secrets together already," she laughed, turning to Jules as she passed out of the door.

Chapter XIV

As soon as Percy Tate confronted his wife at the table that night he saw that something was on her mind.

"You've been to see those circus people," he said.

"How did you know that?"

"Oh, clairvoyance,—my subtle insight into the workings of your brain!"

"I suppose Hawkins told you. Well, I *have* been to see them."

Tate began to pick at the bread beside his plate. He often became preoccupied when he knew his wife wanted him to ask questions; this was his favorite way of teasing her.

"It's the strangest *ménage* I ever saw in my life," Mrs. Tate exclaimed at last, unable to keep back the news any longer. "And it's just as I thought it would be. That poor little creature simply lives in terror of being killed."

Tate rolled his eyes. "'In the midst of life we are in death,'" he said solemnly.

"It's altogether too serious a matter to be made a joke of, Percy. If you could have heard—"

"Now, my dear, you know what I told you. You went to see that woman with the deliberate expectation of finding her a person to be sympathized with, and I can see that you've imagined a lot of nonsense about her. Why in the world don't you let such people alone? You belong in your place and she belongs in hers, and the world is big enough to hold you both without obliging you to come together. You can't understand her feelings any more than she can understand yours. You wonder how you'd feel if you were in her place; you can't realize that if you *were* in her place you'd be an altogether different person. If you had to go through her performances, of course you'd be scared to death; but you forget she's been brought up to do those things; it's her business, her life. I knew you'd go there and work up a lot of ridiculous sympathy, and badger that woman for nothing!"

At the beginning of this speech Mrs. Tate had sat back in her chair with an expression of patient resignation in her face. When her husband finished she breathed a long sigh. "I hope you've said it all, Percy. You're so tiresome when you make those long harangues. Besides, you've only succeeded in showing that you don't understand the case at all."

Then, as they finished their soup, Mrs. Tate gave an account of her call of the afternoon, ending with a graphic repetition of the talk with Blanche about the pains in her back.

"I shall certainly tell Dr. Broughton about it," she cried. "That poor child—she really *is* nothing *but* a child—she's just killing herself by inches, and her husband is worse than a brute to let the thing go on."

"So you want to stop it and take away their only means of support."

"It isn't their only means of support. It seems the husband has money. That makes it all the worse."

"Now, let me say right here, my dear, I wash my hands of this affair. If you want to rush in and upset those people's lives, go ahead, but I'll have nothing to do with it."

"I wish you wouldn't scold me so, Percy. It seems to me I usually bear the consequences of what I do. And I don't see what harm there can be in consulting Dr. Broughton. You're always cracking him up yourself."

Tate burst into a loud laugh. "If that isn't just like a woman! Turning it onto poor old Broughton."

"Oh, sometimes you're so *aggravating*, Percy!"

Two days later, in spite of her husband's opposition, Mrs. Tate consulted Dr. Broughton, and he promised, as soon as he could, to call some morning at the little hotel in Albemarle Street. Before he appeared there Mrs. Tate ingratiated herself into the affections of the family. As Blanche grew more familiar with her, she confided to her many details of her life, and Mrs. Tate speedily possessed the chief facts in connection with it. These facts did not increase her esteem for Jules, whose days, in spite of his duties as his wife's manager, were spent in what she regarded as wholly unpardonable idleness. She also suspected that Jules disliked her; it must have been he who sent word that they would be unable to accept her invitation for dinner on Sunday evening. This, however, did not prevent their being invited for the following Sunday. Mrs. Tate was determined to secure her husband's opinion of her new *protégés*.

Before Sunday came Dr. Broughton unexpectedly made his appearance in the Tates' drawing-room one evening.

"I've seen your acrobat," he said to the figure in yellow silk and lace, reading beside the lamp. "Don't get up. Been out? I hardly thought I'd find you in; you're such a pair of worldlings."

"We came away early. I had a headache," said Tate, shading his eyes with one hand and offering the other to the visitor. "Or, rather, I pretended I had."

The Doctor, a short, stout man of fifty, with grayish brown hair, and little red whiskers jutting out from either side of his face, and with enormous eyebrows shading his keen eyes, gathered his coat-tails in his hand, and took a seat on the couch.

"It's late for a call—must be after ten. But I knew this lady of yours would want to hear about her acrobat. Nice little creature, isn't she? Seems ridiculous she should belong to a circus."

"She doesn't belong there," Mrs. Tate replied, briskly inserting a paper-knife in her book and laying the book on the little table beside her. "I've never seen any one so utterly misplaced. Did you have a talk with her?"

"Yes—a talk. That was all; but that was enough. Her husband was out."

"O, you conspirators!" Tate exclaimed.

"Then you've satisfied yourself about her?" said his wife, ignoring him.

"Yes. She has a very common complaint, a form of meningitis; slumbering meningitis, it's often called. Many people have it without knowing it; and she might have had it even if she hadn't taken to thumping her spine half a dozen times a week. The trouble's located in the spine."

"There, I told you so!" exclaimed Mrs. Tate; and "What a lovely habit women have of never gloating over anything!" her husband added amiably.

"Percy, I wish you'd keep quiet! Do you really think it's serious, Doctor?"

The Doctor held up his hands meditatively, the ends of the fingers touching, and slowly lifted his shoulders. "In itself it may be serious or it may not. Sometimes trouble of that sort is quiescent for years, and the patient dies of something else. Sometimes it resists treatment, and leads to very serious complications,—physical and mental. I've had cases where it has affected the brain and others where it has led to paralysis. In this case it is likely to be aggravated."

"By the diving, you mean?" said Mrs. Tate.

"Exactly. That has probably been the cause of the trouble lately—if it wasn't the first cause. It may go on getting worse, or it may remain as it is for years, or it may disappear for a time, or possibly, altogether."

Mrs. Tate breathed what sounded like a sigh of disappointment. "Then it isn't so bad as I thought," she said.

For a moment the Doctor hesitated. Then he replied: "Yes, it's worse. The mere physical pain that it causes Madame Le Baron is of comparatively little account. I think we may be able to stop that. The peculiarity of the case is the nervousness, the curious fear that seems to haunt her."

In her excitement Mrs. Tate almost bounced from her seat. "That is *exactly* what I said. The poor child hasn't a moment's peace. It's the most terrible thing I ever heard of. And to think that that man—her husband— —"

"It's always the husband," Tate laughed. "Broughton, why don't you stand up for your sex?"

"Percy wants to turn the whole thing into ridicule. I think it's a shame. I can't tell you how it has worried me. I feel so— —"

"For Heaven's sake, Broughton, I wish you'd give my wife something to keep her from feeling for other people. If you don't, she'll go mad, and I shall too. She wants to regulate the whole universe. I have a horrible fear that she's going to get round to me soon."

The Doctor smiled, and bent his bushy eyes on the husband and then on the wife.

"It's a peculiar case," he repeated thoughtfully, when they had sat in silence for several moments. "It couldn't be treated in the ordinary way."

"How in the world did you get so much out of her?" Mrs. Tate asked. "She's the shyest little creature."

"I had to work on her sympathies. I got her to crying,—and then, of course, the whole story came out. As you said, she's haunted by the fear of being killed."

"But that's the baby," said Mrs. Tate quickly. "She told me she never had the least fear till her baby was born."

The Doctor lifted his eyebrows. "It's several things," he replied dryly, refusing to take any but the professional view.

Then they discussed the case in all its aspects. The haunting fear Dr. Broughton regarded as the worst feature. "She says when she goes into the ring, that usually leaves her; but if it came back just before she took her plunge it would kill her. The least miscalculation would be likely to make her land on her head in the net, and that would mean a broken neck. It's terrible work,—that. The law ought to put a stop to it."

"The law ought to put a stop to a good many things that it doesn't," Mrs. Tate snapped. "To think that in this age of civilization— —"

"There she goes, reforming the world again!" her husband interrupted.

"But if the law doesn't stop it in this case," she went on, "*I* will."

For a time they turned from the subject of Blanche and her ills to other themes; but when, about midnight, Dr. Broughton rose to leave, Mrs. Tate went back to it. "We're going to have the Le Barons here for dinner next Sunday," she said. "I wish you'd come in if you can. I want Percy to see what they're like."

"She relies on my judgment after all," said Tate, following the guest to the door. As they stood together in the hall, "You think the case is serious then?" he asked quietly.

The Doctor whispered something in his ear, and Tate nodded thoughtfully. "And how do you think it'll end if she doesn't stop it?"

Dr. Broughton tapped his forehead with his hand. "This is what I'm most afraid of." He seized his stick and thrust it under his arm. "But giving up her performance, I'm afraid, would be like giving up her life. She was practically born in the circus, you know, and I suspect from what your wife has told me that her husband fell in love with her in the circus. Outside of that she seems to have no interest in anything,—except, of course, her family and her baby. But to take her out of the circus would be like pulling up a tree by the roots."

Dr. Broughton was so used to making hurried exits from patients' houses that he lost no time in getting away from Tate. As he went down the steps his host stood with one hand on the knob of the front door, thinking. The Doctor had unconsciously given him a most fascinating suggestion. Around this his mind played as he walked back to the drawing-room, where his wife was yawning, and gathering, some books to take upstairs. He said nothing to her about it; before expressing his fancy, he decided to wait until he saw those curious people.

Chapter XV

Mrs. Tate was right in surmising that Jules had conceived a dislike for her. The first day he saw her he decided that she was a tiresome, interfering Englishwoman, and he watched with annoyance her growing intimacy with Blanche, whom he wished to keep wholly to himself. Of his wife's success at the Hippodrome he felt as proud as if it were his own; he loved to read the notices of it in the papers, and while Blanche was performing, to walk about in the audience and hear her praises. He had come to look upon her as part of himself, as his property; and this sense of proprietorship added to the fascination that her performance had for him.

Though his first ardor of devotion had passed, he was still tender with her; but his tenderness always had reference more to her work than to herself. He watched her as the owner of a performing animal might have watched his precious charge. Sometimes he used to lose patience with her for her devotion to the little Jeanne; if Jeanne cried at night she would want to leave the bed to soothe her. In order to prevent this, Jules had the child's crib moved into Madeleine's room, to the secret grief of the mother, who, however, did not think of resisting his commands. In his way Jules was fond of Jeanne; but he could not help thinking that before she came Blanche had given all her love to him. However, there was some excuse for that; but there was no reason why a stranger like Mrs. Tate should come in and take possession of them, act like a member of the family, and put a lot of silly ideas into his wife's head.

The mere fact that Mrs. Tate was English would have been enough to prejudice Jules against her even if he had not objected to her personal qualities. He hated the English, and he hated England, especially London. Even Blanche, who was blind to his faults, speedily discovered that his boast of being a born traveller had no foundation in fact. On arriving in London he had gone straight to a French hotel, where he was served to French cooking by a *garçon* trained in the *cafés* of the *Boulevards*. Since then he had associated only with the few French people he could find in the city; if he hadn't been eager to read everything printed about Blanche, he would never have looked at any but French papers. At home he spent a large part of his time in ridiculing the English, just as on his return from America he had ridiculed the Americans. Now, at the thought of being obliged to dine with a lot of those *bêtes d'Anglais* he felt enraged. He had already refused one invitation. Why wasn't that enough for them? The second he would have refused too, if Blanche had not insisted that another refusal would be a discourtesy to Father Dumény's friends. Ah, Father Dumény, a fine box he had got them into, the tiresome old woman that he was, with his foolish jokes and his rheumatism!

Jules never forgot that dinner. In the first place, he was awed by the magnificence of the Tates' house; it surpassed anything of the kind he had ever seen in France or in America; it had never occurred to him that the English could have such good taste. Then, too, in spite of the efforts of his hosts to make him comfortable, he felt awkward, ill at ease, out of place. As soon as he entered the drawing-room, Blanche was taken upstairs by Mrs. Tate, and Jules was left with the husband and with Dr. Broughton.

A moment later the Doctor disappeared, and for the next half-hour Jules tried to maintain a conversation in English. Tate turned the conversation to life in Paris as compared with the life of London, but Jules had so much difficulty in speaking English that they fell at last into French.

Meanwhile, Blanche sat in the library with Mrs. Tate and Dr. Broughton, whom she had not seen since the day of his call upon her. The Doctor had at once won her confidence, and since her talk with him she had felt better, and she fancied that the tonic he gave her had already benefited her. But she still had that pain in her back, she said, and that terrible fear; every night when she kissed the little Jeanne before going to the Hippodrome, she felt as if she should never see the child again. If she didn't stop feeling like that, she didn't know what would happen.

"If you could give up the plunge for a while," the Doctor suggested, "you'd be very much better for the rest. Then you might go back to it, you know."

"But I'm engaged for the season," Blanche replied in French, which the Doctor readily understood, but refused to speak. "I can't break my contract."

"Perhaps you could make a compromise," Mrs. Tate suggested. "You could go on with your trapeze performance,—with everything except the dive."

"I was really engaged for that," said Blanche, a look of dismay appearing in her face. "There are many others that perform on the trapeze."

"But you might try to make some arrangement," Mrs. Tate insisted. "Your husband could talk it over with the managers."

"Ah, but he would not like it," Blanche replied with evident distress. "It would make him so unhappy if he—if he knew."

"If he knew you were being made ill by your work!" Mrs. Tate interrupted. "Of course it would make him unhappy, and it would be very strange if it didn't. But it's much better to have him know it than for you to go on risking your life every night."

Dr. Broughton gave his hostess a glance that made her quail. A moment later, however, she gathered herself together.

"I didn't mean to say that, dear, but now that I *have* said it, there's no use mincing matters. The Doctor has told me plainly that if you go on making that plunge every night in your present state of nervousness it will certainly result in your death—in one way or another. So the only thing for you to do, for the sake of your baby, and your husband, and for your own sake too,—the only thing for you to do is to stop it, at least for a time. If you were to break your neck it would simply be murder,—yes, murder," she repeated, glancing at the Doctor, who was looking at her with an expression that showed he thought she was going too far.

Tears had begun to trickle down Blanche's cheeks, and now they turned to sobs. For a few moments she lost control of herself, and her frail figure was shaken with grief. Dr. Broughton said nothing, and he looked angry. Mrs. Tate paid no attention to him; she went over to Blanche, took her in her arms, and began to soothe her. In a few moments the sobbing ceased, and Mrs. Tate went on:—

"It's best that you should know this, dear, though perhaps I've been cruel in telling it to you so bluntly. We must tell your husband about it, too. I'm sure he'll be distressed to hear how much you've suffered, and he'll be glad to do anything that will help you. So now we'll send the Doctor away, and bathe your face with hot water, and go down to dinner and try to forget about our troubles for a while."

If Jules had not been absorbed in his own embarrassment at the dinner-table he might have discovered traces of agitation in his wife's face. He was secretly execrating the luck that had brought him among these people, and he resolved when he returned home to tell Blanche that he would have nothing more to do with them. If she was willing to have that prying Englishwoman about her all the time, she could, but she mustn't expect him to be more than civil to her. The conversation had turned on English politics, and as Jules had nothing to offer on the subject, his enforced silence increased his discomfort. Mrs. Tate was devoting herself to Blanche, who sat beside her, relating in French stories of her life in Paris. Jules felt resentful; no one paid attention to him; when he dined out in Paris he was always one of the leaders in the talk. He wanted to justify himself, to show these people that he was no fool, that he was worthy of being the husband of a celebrity.

By a fortunate chance, the talk drifted to American politics, and Jules, seeing his opportunity, seized it. A few moments later he was launched on an account of his travels in the United States. Tate, relieved at having at last found a topic his guest could discuss, gave Jules full play, and listened to him with a light in his eyes that showed his wife he was secretly amused. Indeed, Jules' criticisms of America and his descriptions of the peculiarities of Americans greatly entertained them.

The dinner closed in animated talk, much to the relief of Mrs. Tate, who feared it would be a great failure; it made her realize, however, that as show people the Le Barons were quite useless. She was afraid Blanche had been bored; she had been sitting almost speechless during the meal, sighing heavily now and then, as if thinking that in a few hours her respite would be over, and she would have to return to her horrible work.

Mrs. Tate was quite ready to make any sacrifice to rescue Blanche from the terrors of her circus life; in the enthusiasm of the moment she said to herself, that rather than let her continue making that plunge, she would offer to *pay* her husband what she earned, in order to take his wife out of the ring altogether. At the thought of persuading him to do this, Mrs. Tate felt that at last she had a definite task to perform; it was almost like a mission, and the harder it proved to be, the more exalted she would feel.

After their return to the drawing-room, Mrs. Tate, with a delightful feeling that she was engaged in a conspiracy, made a mysterious sign to Dr. Broughton to come to her.

"I suppose Percy's been whispering to you not to have anything to do with this scheme of mine, but don't pay any attention to him. Do you know, I think the best way would be to take the husband into the library and have it out there. He must *be* told, you know. He hasn't a suspicion of it,—not a suspicion. You wait a few minutes, and as soon as I get a chance, I'll ask him to follow me out."

The Doctor smiled and shrugged his shoulders.

"You must take the responsibility," he said carelessly. "I shall merely do my professional duty. Mr. Tate has just been telling me about a curious idea——"

"Don't pay any attention to his ideas. Percy thinks everything ought to be left to regulate itself. A fine world it would be if every one thought as he does. Now you go back to him, and follow me when I tell you. No, I have a better plan. You go into the library with Percy. I'll come in there in a few minutes."

A quarter of an hour later, when Mrs. Tate entered the library with Jules, she found her husband and the Doctor there, half-hidden in a cloud of smoke.

"This poor man, too, has been dying for another cigar," she said; "but he's too polite to say so. So while he's smoking we can have our talk. We'll take our coffee in here, too. Percy, you go and see that Madame Le Baron is properly served. I've had to leave her there alone for a minute, but I said I'd send you in. Dr. Broughton and I are going to have a secret conference with Monsieur Le Baron."

"Secret conferences are always dangerous," Tate replied, rising to leave the room. "Look out for them!" he added with a smile to Jules, as he hesitated at the door. When he had closed the door behind him, he stood in the hall a moment, thinking.

Tate was a man of sense, of "horse-sense," one of his friends used to say of him, and not given to forebodings. Now, however, he had a distinct regret that his wife was interfering in this matter, and fear of the consequences. She often did things that he disapproved, and he made no objection, for he believed that she had as much right to independence as himself; but in this case he would have liked to interfere. He had spoken to Dr. Broughton about his feeling in the matter, and the Doctor had merely laughed. Well, the Doctor knew better than he did; perhaps, after all, his own theory was absurd. At any rate, he could not be held accountable for any trouble that might result from his wife's meddling. This thought, however, gave him little consolation. He usually suffered for her mistakes much more than she did herself.

When he went back to the drawing-room, he had difficulty in sustaining a conversation with Blanche; he kept thinking of the conference in the next room, wondering what the result would be. He was prepared to see Jules enter with a pale face and set lips and with wrath in his eyes.

When Jules finally entered between his hostess and the Doctor, Tate scanned his face narrowly; it was not white, and the lips were not set, but the whole expression had changed to a look of dogged determination and ill-concealed rage. He sat near his wife, staring at her as if he had never seen her before.

For a few moments the conversation was resumed, but the atmosphere seemed chilled. Then the Doctor rose to say good-night, explaining that he had promised to call on a patient in Curzon Street before going home. This seemed to be the signal for the breaking-up, and all of the guests left at the same moment, Mrs. Tate calling out to Blanche at the door of the drawing-room that she would look in on her the next day if she were not too busy.

When the front door had closed, Tate turned to his wife.

"Well, you had a stormy time of it, didn't you?"

She walked toward the centre of the drawing-room and stood under the chandelier, keeping her eyes fixed on her husband's face, which seemed to be much more serious than usual.

"What makes you think so?" she asked, removing a bracelet from her arm and nervously twirling it.

"I could tell from the expression in his eyes, and from the way you and the Doctor acted. He was furious, wasn't he?"

"Furious? Le Baron? Hardly; though I could see he didn't believe a word we said. He was almost too startled to understand it at first. The little goose hadn't said a word to him about it."

"And what did he say when you told him she ought to give up her performance? How did he like that?"

"He didn't like it at all, apparently. But I didn't expect him to like it. It means money out of his pocket."

"No, it means more than that, if I'm not mistaken."

"What else can it mean?" she said, lifting her eyebrows questioningly.

"It means the end of whatever affection he has for his wife. Of course he never had much. A man of his sort doesn't."

She looked at him with curiosity in her face. "What difference does her performing make in his affection for her?"

"Can't you see that he didn't fall in love with *her*? He fell in love with her performance."

Mrs. Tate put one finger to her lips and hesitated for a moment. Then she said slowly:—

"How ridiculous you are, Percy! As if any one ever heard of such a thing!"

Chapter XVI

On the way home in the hansom that he had called, Jules scarcely spoke. Blanche kept glancing at him covertly; she had never before seen that look in his face, and it alarmed her; he seemed to be trying to keep back the anger that showed itself in his half-closed eyes and his firm-set chin. When they reached the lodgings, Blanche found Madeleine sound asleep by the fireplace, and without waking her, she started to go into the next room to see if Jeanne were comfortable. When she reached the door, Jules said in a low voice:—

"Wait here a minute. I have something to say to you."

At the sound of the words, Madeleine's eyes opened slowly, and she blinked at Jules, who was glancing angrily at her.

"This is a pretty way you take care of Jeanne. She might have had a dozen convulsions without your knowing anything about them."

In spite of Jules' command, the reference to the convulsions, which had nearly cost Jeanne her life a few weeks after birth, sent Blanche agitatedly into the nursery. Madeleine lumbered behind her, and both were relieved to find the child sleeping contentedly in her cradle, her cheeks flushed, and her chubby hands clenched at her breast. Blanche would have liked to pass several moments there in rapt adoration, but Jules appeared at the door and made a sign to her to come to him.

"Madeleine will look out for her," he said, pointing to the cradle. "Go to bed, Madeleine."

Blanche tiptoed out of the room, removed her wraps, and, with the overcoat Jules had thrown on the couch, hung them in the little closet beside the big mirror. Jules, who had taken a seat in front of the fire-place, watched her impatiently, and then motioned her to sit in the chair opposite him.

"Now perhaps you'll be kind enough to tell me what all this means. I knew that Englishwoman would be up to some mischief. What does it mean?" he said sternly.

Blanche looked timidly into his face; the expression of anger that she had noticed on their way home was still there. She did not know what to say, and tears of misery filled her eyes and rolled slowly down her cheeks.

Then weakened by her previous outburst, she covered her face with her hands, and began to sob, giving expression to all the torture that had come from the horror of her performance, from her incessant terror of being killed and separated from Jeanne. Jules was at first touched, and then alarmed, by the unexpected display of grief.

He waited, thinking that it would soon expend itself; then when the sobs continued, he went over to her, and taking her gently in his arms, tried to soothe her by stroking her hair and calling her by the endearing names he had used during the first weeks of their marriage, and begging her to control herself for his sake, it hurt him so. After this last appeal, Blanche put her arms round his neck, and buried her head on his breast, and for a few moments they sat together without speaking, her body shaken now and then from the violence of her grief. Then Jules began to question her quietly, and the whole story of her sufferings since Jeanne's birth came out so pathetically that, in spite of his anger, he was touched, and convinced that, after all, the Englishwoman had been right.

In his remorse that Blanche had suffered in silence, and he had not found it out, had done nothing to help her, he declared he would have the diving stopped at once, no matter what the cost might be. Rather than see her unhappy, he would make her give up performing altogether, if that were necessary. At any rate, he would go to Marshall the next day and see what could be done about taking her name off the bills. They would leave this disgusting London, perhaps for the south of France, where Blanche could have a long rest, and gather strength for her visit to America the next year. For a long time they talked over the plan, and then Jules made Blanche go to bed.

"You'll not be able to do your work tomorrow," he said, "if you sit up much longer. Of course, you can't stop it at once. Marshall wouldn't listen to that. You're his best attraction, and he'll have to advertise your last appearances."

For more than an hour after Blanche left him, Jules walked up and down the little drawing-room, smoking cigarettes. The revelation of his wife's trouble had so upset him that he felt unable to sleep. But it was of himself, not of her, that he was chiefly thinking. Dr. Broughton had told him that a long rest might cure Blanche of her nervous terror and relieve her of the pains in the back, but it was probable that she would be affected again as soon as she resumed her performance.

If this proved true, his own career would be ruined; there would be no more travelling, no more triumphs! Blanche would sink into obscurity, would become a mere nonentity, devoted to her child and house-keeping, like scores of other wives and mothers that he knew and despised in Paris. Out of the circus, she was utterly commonplace, Jules said to himself, and the fact came to him with the force of a revelation! But for that he would never have married her; the brilliancy of her talent had dazzled him! And now, if she had to leave the circus, how beautifully he would have been tricked! He would be tied down to her and her child! The expense of maintaining them would oblige him to live meanly, in a way that he had never been used to, that he loathed.

What a fine trap he had got himself into! There was absolutely no escape, unless Blanche recovered from her ridiculous cowardice. And all on account of that infant, who had come into the world without being wanted, and had spoiled his life! For the moment Jules hated Jeanne. He wished she had never been born, or had died at birth; then all this trouble wouldn't have occurred. But for Jeanne, Blanche might have accepted that offer for a summer season at Trouville. Then he wouldn't have been bored at Boulogne, and Father Dumény wouldn't have given him that letter to those beasts of English.

Then Jules' wrath turned from Jeanne to Father Dumény, and on him he poured all his old bitterness against priests. They were always interfering, those black-coated, oily-tongued hypocrites. Oh, if he had Father Dumény there! He would have liked to choke him!

The more Jules thought, the more convinced he became that his wife's nervousness was due to imagination rather than to any physical cause. Then, too, Blanche had been homesick after her long stay in Boulogne, where she saw her mother and her sisters every day. What a fool he had been to allow her to go there! He hated the whole pack of them—Father Dumény, Madame Berthier, her tiresome old husband, all! What right did they have to interfere with Blanche? She was his wife, she belonged to him alone. When he reached this point Jules had worked himself into a fine indignation; but he had exhausted his cigarettes, and it was now nearly twelve o'clock. Instead of going to bed, however, he threw himself on the couch in the corner of the room, where a few hours later Blanche found him, sleeping soundly.

Jules woke in an irritable mood, cross with Madeleine, indifferent to Jeanne, with whom he usually liked to gambol after breakfast, and silent with his wife. For a time he said nothing to Blanche about their talk of the night before, and the expression of his face prevented her from touching upon it. Till eleven o'clock he was busily engaged in writing letters; when he had finished these, he turned to Blanche, who was sitting alone by the table, making a dress for Jeanne.

"I've just written to Hicks in New York," he said, "the man who made me that fine offer for next September. I told him we couldn't sign the contract yet. That'll probably make him offer us more money, and it'll give you time to find out whether you can go on with your work again."

"But I shall surely go on with it," said Blanche, hardly daring to look into his face. "I shall be well again after a rest. I know I shall. The Doctor said—"

"Never mind what the Doctor said. I don't believe he knows anything about it. You're just a little nervous, that's all. You worry about little things too much, about Jeanne especially. Why can't you let Madeleine take care of Jeanne? She knows a good deal more about children than you do. That's what we pay her for. The child costs us enough, Heaven knows, and if your salary's going to be cut off, we'll have to be pretty economical."

For a moment Blanche said nothing; her lips quivered, but she controlled herself. Jules looked at her narrowly, and said to himself that she was not half so pretty as she had been; she was growing thinner, and there were little lines in her face that ought not to be in the face of one so young as her mother said she was. How weak, how helpless she seemed! Once the thought of her weakness and ingenuousness had given him pleasure; now it only made him realize his own superiority.

"Perhaps," she suggested hesitatingly,—"perhaps Mr. Marshall might be willing to make a new contract. Perhaps he would let me go on with my performance on the trapeze and the rope—without the dive."

"I've thought of that," Jules replied, rising and going to the closet for his overcoat. "But it isn't at all likely. He's been advertising your dive all over London, and it's been his best feature. He'll be pretty mad when I tell him you're going to give it up. He'll probably try to make me pay a forfeit for breach of contract."

"For breach of contract!" she repeated blankly. "I—"

"Oh, don't worry about it," said Jules, with a pang of regret for the pain he had caused her. "I think I can make that all right. I suppose that old Doctor would write a certificate if I asked him."

He drew on the fur-lined coat, and as he took his gloves from his pocket he started for the door, without kissing Blanche. Then, at the door, glancing back, and seeing her standing in the middle of the room with a look of helpless pain in her face, he turned and walked towards her, and bent his face to hers.

"There, there, dear, don't worry," he said. "You'll be all right again in a little while!" At the door he added: "I shall be back in an hour or two, and tell you what Marshall says."

The hour or two proved to be three hours, and these Blanche passed chiefly in walking up and down the apartment. She could not keep still; she felt convinced that something dreadful was going to happen. She hardly dared even to talk to Jeanne, as if she fancied the child might divine her misery. She feared that she would be unable to give up her performance, and she feared she would have to go on with it. If she did give it up, she had a presentiment that she would pay dear for the release; if she did not, she knew it would result in her death.

Ever since coming to London, she had prepared herself for the catastrophe. No one, not even kind-hearted Mrs. Tate, could imagine the agony of mind she had endured. And it was all for Jeanne! Her very sufferings had fed her love for the child. If she and Jules could go away with Jeanne, far away, where they would never hear or think of performances again, how happy they would be! But she must go on with her work; she ought to fight against her weakness. Jules had said she would grow strong again; she had always believed what he said, and perhaps he was right now. Perhaps after a rest she would want to go back to the ring. But she was afraid, she was afraid! Poor little Jeanne! Every few moments she ran into the room where Jeanne was taking her mid-day sleep. She wanted to clasp the child to her breast and walk up and down the room with her. But for several weeks she had not dared to hold her in her arms for fear of dropping her from nervousness.

Instead of going directly to the Hippodrome, Jules turned into Piccadilly, where he had seen the sign of a French physician. He had suddenly decided to seek further medical advice before speaking to Marshall, and he did not propose to trust Blanche's case to another Englishman. He was obliged to wait in Dr. Viaud's outer office for more than an hour. The Doctor received him with what seemed to Jules an almost suspicious courtesy; but this disappeared as soon as he explained that he was French.

Jules was gratified by the interest paid to his repetition of Blanche's confession of the night before. The Doctor did not interrupt till Jules had mentioned the advice given by the English physician.

"Broughton!" he exclaimed, repeating the name after Jules. "You couldn't have consulted a better man. He's at the head of his profession here in London."

When he had questioned Jules about Blanche's symptoms, he said thoughtfully: "I cannot add anything to the advice Dr. Broughton has given,—that is, of course, with my present knowledge of the case. But I have absolute confidence in his judgment. The pains in the back I do not fear so much as the terrible apprehension that you say haunts your wife. In itself that is, of course, great suffering; and the consequences may be fatal. Your wife's dive requires iron nerve, and that is being constantly weakened by her continual worrying. I agree with Dr. Broughton that she at least needs a rest as soon as possible. There can't be two opinions about that. But I should not like to interfere with Dr. Broughton's—"

Jules understood at once, and rose from his seat.

"I merely wanted to see what you thought. If you had disagreed—"

"Ah, but Dr. Broughton is very reliable!" said the Frenchman, with a smile and a shrug, as if afraid of even a suggestion of professional discourtesy.

Jules left him feeling bitterly disappointed. There was no hope then! He had surmised that the shrewd-eyed Englishman knew his business. There was nothing to do but to go to Marshall and explain the situation.

When he returned from the Hippodrome to the apartment Blanche met him at the door. His face was darkened with a scowl.

"What did he say?" she asked nervously, as he entered and threw his overcoat on a chair. "Was he—was he angry?"

"Angry? No; he was altogether too cool. If he'd been angry I shouldn't have cared. I'd have liked that a good deal better."

"Then we sha'n't have to pay a forfeit?" said Blanche, glancing up into his face.

He turned away and threw himself wearily on the couch. "No, you won't have to pay a forfeit, but you'll have to go on with the engagement."

"With the diving?" she said, her face growing white.

"No, with the other work—on the trapeze and the rope. He said you'd have to elaborate that, and he'd pay you half what you're getting now till you were ready to do the diving again. He wants to keep you on account of your name. He's advertised you all over the city, and even out in the country places near London."

"But he—he doesn't object to my giving up the plunge?" Blanche repeated, in a tone which suggested that her professional pride was hurt.

"He didn't when I told him the Doctor had forbidden your going on with it for a while. Besides, he had another reason for not objecting."

"What was that?"

"He showed me a letter he'd just had from that woman who made such a sensation in Bucharest while we were in Vienna. Don't you remember? I showed you some of her notices. She does a swimming act, and dives from a platform into a tank. She's been playing in the English provinces, and now she wants to come to London."

"So he's going to engage her in my place?" Blanche gasped.

"In your place?" Jules repeated irritably. "How can he engage her in your place when he's going to keep you? We've got to live, and it won't hurt you to go on with your work on the trapeze and the rope. He knows your name will be an attraction, and if he engages that Englishwoman, she'll be another card for him—a big one. He says she's been drawing crowds in Manchester for six weeks."

"What's her name?"

"King—Lottie King—or something like that."

"Is she pretty? Did he show you her pictures?"

"Yes; her manager sent him a whole box of them. She's *petite*, with wicked little eyes."

"Dark?"

"No, blonde."

"And what is her dive?"

"What?"

"How high is it?"

"Fifty feet, Marshall said; but one of the circus hands told me it wasn't much more, than forty."

"Oh!" There was a suggestion of a sneer in her tone, and Jules looked up in surprise.

"Of course, it's nothing compared with yours," he said, to console her.

"When is she going to begin?" she asked, after a moment.

"Going to begin? Do you mean here in London? Marshall hasn't signed with her yet. She's engaged in Manchester for three weeks longer."

"Then I shall have to go on with my dive till she comes?"

"I suppose so," Jules replied coldly.

She saw that he did not wish to continue the conversation; so she went into the nursery, leaving him lying on the couch, where he often took an afternoon nap; since coming to London he had grown very lazy, and had gained flesh. Blanche found Jeanne wide awake and crowing in Madeleine's arms. She sat beside the cradle, and taking the child in her lap, sent Madeleine out of the room. Jeanne snatched at the brooch she wore at her throat, and laughed into her face. Blanche tried to smile in reply, but the tears welled into her eyes again, and fell in big drops on her cheeks.

Chapter XVII

Three days after Jules' talk with Marshall, the forthcoming engagement at the Hippodrome of Miss Lottie King was announced in the London newspapers. Blanche signed a new contract, by which she agreed to perform for several weeks longer on the trapeze and on the rope at half the salary she had been receiving. Marshall said that no mention of the plunge would be made in the papers; her name would continue to "draw," and the public would be satisfied with Miss King's great dive into the tank. This remark made Jules very angry, and it also depressed Blanche, who felt as if she had already been deposed from her supremacy as the chief attraction at the Hippodrome. Indeed, as the time drew near when she was to cease making the plunge, instead of feeling happier, she grew more despondent; she had already elaborated her performance on the trapeze by introducing several new feats that she and Jules had planned together, but with these she was not satisfied; she felt like an actor obliged to play small parts after winning success in leading characters.

As for Jules, he did not try to hide his discontent at the change in his wife's work. In the first place, it made his brief but dramatic public appearance unnecessary; in future he would be obliged to conduct Blanche to the circus, and live again like any mere hanger-on to the skirts of a public performer. The *rôle* was ignoble, unworthy of him. Then, too, he chafed at the thought of his wife's decline in importance at the Hippodrome; he fancied that when her inability to go on with the plunge had become known to the other performers they would lose respect for her and for himself.

He secretly doubted if the public would accept Blanche merely for her performance on the trapeze and on the rope. Almost any one could do that; but in the plunge she was without a rival. He hoped that, as a compensation for his vexation, the performance of Miss King would be a failure. Forty feet! What did that amount to in comparison with the magnificent plunge of more than ninety feet that Blanche had made at Vienna?

Already Jules had begun to think of his wife in the past tense chiefly, as if she lived in the triumphs she had made by her nightly flight through the air. Indeed, she seemed to him almost another person now. Instead of looking on her almost with reverence, as he had done, he felt sorry for her, as if she were his inferior; and though he continued to treat her with kindness, there was a suggestion of pity, almost of contempt, in his manner toward her. She sought consolation in her child, who, she thought, grew stronger and more beautiful every day. For Jeanne's sake she tried to be glad the time was so near when she should give up risking her life; but the nearer it grew, the more depressed she became, and the more she thought about that woman who was to take her place.

Mrs. Tate, who had definitely taken Blanche under her protection, and called at the little hotel several times each week, had been delighted at what she considered the fortunate solution of a shocking difficulty. Now that Blanche was to stop making that horrible dive, there was no reason why she shouldn't be the happiest woman in the world. With her keen instinct, however, she observed that Blanche was not happy; she wondered, too, at the frequent absence of the husband from this *ménage*. Jules couldn't be very devoted, she thought, for a man who had been married little more than a year. Perhaps, however, he avoided her; for, in spite of his French politeness, he had not been able to conceal his dislike for her. For this reason she did not ask him to dinner again. She often took Blanche and Jeanne to drive in the afternoon, and pointed out the celebrities that they passed in the Park.

"My husband says I take you to drive just to show you off," she said jokingly one day. "He thinks I have a mania for celebrities."

"Ah, but I'm not a celebrity!" Blanche replied, with a smile that was almost sad.

"Not a celebrity? Of course you are. I haven't a doubt that half the people we meet recognize you. You know, it's been quite the fashion to go to the Hippodrome this year."

"But I sha'n't be a celebrity much longer," said Blanche, glancing at the bare boughs of the trees, and wondering if any other place could be as desolate as London in winter.

"Why not? You don't think of retiring into private life altogether, do you?" Mrs. Tate laughed.

"No, but I shall only be an ordinary performer after this week."

"But I'd rather be an ordinary performer and keep my neck whole than be an *ex*traordinary one and risk my life every night," Mrs. Tate retorted sharply. She was vexed with Blanche for not appreciating her emancipation.

They rode on in silence for a few moments. Then Blanche said,—

"There's some one going to take my place, you know."

"Some one that's going to make that dreadful plunge?" Mrs. Tate cried in horror.

"No, not that. She jumps into a tank of water—from a platform—only about forty feet. My jump is more than seventy-five feet," Blanche added with a touch of pride.

Mrs. Tate rested her hands in her lap and burst out laughing. "What a ridiculous thing! I beg your pardon, dear, but I can't help being amused. Of course it doesn't seem funny to you. You're used to it; but it does to me."

Then she questioned Blanche about the new performer, and Blanche repeated what Jules had told her and what she had since heard of the woman at the Hippodrome. Mrs. Tate was greatly interested, and laughed immoderately; afterward, however, when she had returned home and thought over the conversation, she regarded it more seriously.

"What do you think, Percy?" she said at the dinner table that night. "Those Hippodrome people have engaged a creature to dive into a tank of water from a platform. Of course, that's to take the place of Madame Le Baron's plunge. Could anything be more absurd? The worst of it is that the poor little woman is frightfully jealous already. I could see that from the way she talked. What a dreadful world it is, isn't it? They're all like that, aren't they, even the best of them? Do you remember that poor Madame Gardini who sang here one night? She told me if she had her life to live over again she'd never dream of going on the stage. She said opera-singers were the unhappiest people in the world,—just poisoned with jealousy. And these circus people are exactly like them!"

"What makes you think she's jealous? What was it she said?"

"It wasn't *what* she said, it was the *way* she talked about the woman. Her husband says she's a great beauty."

"Ah, the husband says so, does he?" Tate remarked dryly. A moment later he added: "I wish you hadn't had anything to do with those people!"

"You've said that a dozen times, Percy, and I wish you'd stop. For my part, I'm very glad I've met them. If I hadn't, that poor little creature would be in her grave before the end of a year."

"Perhaps she'll wish that she *were* in her grave before the end of the year."

"What do you mean by that?"

"Nothing, dear, nothing. Don't catch at everything I say. How is she now—any better? I suppose she's easier in mind now that she's going to stop that diving?"

"That's the strangest thing about it," Mrs. Tate answered, with a change of tone. "I thought she would be, too, but she isn't. I really believe she's sorry she's giving it up. But perhaps that's because she's been doing it all her life. She'll miss it at first—even if it did worry her nearly to death!"

"Has Dr. Broughton been to see her lately?"

"No; he said it wouldn't be necessary. He's going to wait to see what effect the rest from the diving will have on her."

For a few moments Tate looked thoughtfully at his wife. "Upon my word," he said, "I half suspect that you *want* something to happen to that little woman. It would just be romantic enough to suit you."

"Percy, how can you talk so? You're simply brutal."

"She might at least break a leg to please you," her husband laughed, "before giving up that plunge."

Blanche made her last dive without the accident that Tate had regarded as indispensable to dramatic effect. Indeed, since knowing that she was to give it up, she seemed to have lost much of her terror of the plunge; she thought of it now chiefly with regret. That night, as she rode home with Jules and Madeleine, she seemed depressed; Jules, too, was even more sullen than he had been for the past two weeks. When they had entered the lodgings and were eating their midnight meal, she said:—

"If to-morrow is pleasant we might take Jeanne for a drive in the country. The air would do her good."

"I can't go," he replied indifferently. "I have something else to do. Besides, it would cost too much. We shall have to be economical now that you're going to be on half-salary."

The next morning Jules left the hotel at eleven o'clock, saying that he shouldn't be back for luncheon. He did not explain where he was going, and Blanche did not question him. She busied herself with Jeanne, and this distracted her till Jeanne fell sound asleep. Then she became a prey to her old melancholy, and for an hour she walked up and down the room, to the bewilderment of Madeleine, who could not understand what the matter was.

"Is Madame suffering with the pain in her back?" Madeleine asked at last.

No, Madame was not suffering. She had not been troubled by the pain for several days; she hoped it would leave her for good now that she had stopped taking the plunge.

"Ah, God be praised that you do that no longer!" Madeleine cried, lifting her withered hands to heaven and rolling her eyes. "It was too terrible. Since that first night in Paris, when I went with you and Monsieur Jules, I never dared to look. It was *affreux*!"

"But Jules loved it," said Blanche, throwing herself into a chair beside the old woman.

Ah, yes, Madeleine acknowledged. He used to rave about it in the little flat in the *rue de Lisbonne.* Once Madeleine heard him talking in his sleep about the circus and the wonderful dive; he always slept with his door wide-open, and she often heard him talking away like one wide-awake. He had told her that it was the most wonderful thing he had ever seen, and no other woman in the world would have dared to do it. Madeleine was always delighted to have a chance to talk about Jules, and she babbled on, never suspecting that her words were making Blanche suffer.

"Do you think," Blanche said at last, "do you think he would have loved me if I hadn't done that—if I hadn't done that plunge, I mean—in the Circus?"

Madeleine glanced at her quickly; she was unable to grasp the significance of the question. "But he did see you in the Circus," she replied. "If he hadn't seen you there, *chérie,* he wouldn't have seen you at all."

"Yes, yes, that's true." Blanche realized that it would be useless to try to explain what she meant. Then, after a moment, she added, "And now that I've given up the dive,—perhaps I shall never be able to do it again; the Doctor said I might not,—now that I've given it up, do you think he'll love me just the same?"

Madeleine's faded eyes turned to Blanche and examined her closely. "If he'll love you just the same?" she repeated. "What has put such a strange idea into your head, child? Of course he'll love you just the same."

Then Madeleine was launched on a flood of eulogy. Jules was so good, so faithful, so affectionate. There was not another like him. He had always been so tender with his mother; and oh, how his poor mother had worshipped him! Madeleine's praises had the effect of soothing Blanche for a time; they also made her ashamed of the half-conscious suspicion which had arisen in her mind, and which she would not have dared to formulate even to herself. She only permitted herself to acknowledge that his present manner toward her was different from his old one. She was also disturbed by his refusal for the past three Sundays to go to church with her.

The next afternoon Jules came home in a rage. "I've been down to see Marshall," he said. "What do you suppose the old fool's gone and done? He had the door of your dressing-room opened this morning and all your things turned out into Miss Van Pelt's old room,—the little hole next door, you know. It's hardly big enough to breathe in. He said you weren't the star any longer, and he must give the room to Miss King. It seems she's a kicker and he's afraid of a row."

Blanche had nothing to say in reply; this seemed to her only another indignity added to those she had already suffered. The worst was to come in the evening, when her rival would share the applause that used to be hers. A few moments later she asked,—

"Was she there—that woman?"

"No; she hasn't appeared yet, and Marshall was a little nervous. She was to come up from Manchester in a train that got in during the afternoon."

"But suppose she doesn't come."

"Oh, she'll come fast enough. Marshall had a telegram saying she'd started. Her big iron tub arrived this morning. They were putting it in the ground and laying the pipes for the water when I was there. They keep it covered till her act begins."

"What does she do besides her jump?"

"Oh, Marshall says she goes through a lot of antics, stays under the water till she nearly dies of suffocation, and cooks a meal, and—"

"Under water?" Blanche gasped.

"No, of course not, you ninny," Jules cried impatiently. His wife's simplicity had long before ceased to amuse him. "She does it while she's floating. Then one of the circus boys falls into the tank, and she shows how she used to rescue people out in California."

"Then she's an American."

"She's lived in America all her life, but her father was an Englishman, and she was born in England. Her father kept a swimming school out in San Francisco; that's how she got into the business. They say she's got a lot of medals for saving lives."

As Jules walked into the next room to change his clothes for the evening, he said to himself that his wife was growing very stupid and tiresome.

Blanche sat alone for a few moments, feeling cold and forlorn. She could not keep from thinking and wondering about that woman; she was anxious and yet afraid to see her. She could not account for the dislike and terror with which the mere thought of the woman inspired her. She had never before regarded the other performers in the circus as her rivals; so, for the first time in her life, she knew the bitterness of jealousy.

Before preparing for the evening she went into the nursery, and for several moments sat beside the cradle where Jeanne was peacefully sleeping, her little face rosy with health. The poor child, she thought, could never know the sacrifice she had made for her. She was glad she had made it; she had done her duty; but it was hard, it was so hard! Then she bent over and kissed Jeanne on the cheek; the child drew her head away, and buried her face impatiently in the pillow. Blanche turned her gently in the crib, adjusted the lace covering, and stole out of the room.

Jules met her as she was closing the door softly behind her. "What have you been doing in there?" he cried petulantly. "Why can't you let Jeanne alone when she's asleep? Every time she takes a nap you go in and wake her up. No wonder—"

"I haven't waked her," Blanche replied apologetically. "I only went in to see if she needed anything, and I sat beside her a moment."

"Well, you'll spoil her if you keep on. From the way you act one would imagine that Jeanne was the only creature in the world worth thinking about!"

They both took their places at the table which Madeleine had prepared, and proceeded silently with their dinner. Madeleine, who hovered about them, wondered what the matter was; she had never seen Monsieur Jules like this before; he usually had a great deal to say. When she had left the room for a few minutes, Jules looked up from his plate.

"I've been wondering whether we ought to keep Madeleine or not. She's a great expense. We could get along just as well without her. The *garçon* could serve our meals. We have to pay for the service whether we get it or not."

When he had spoken he was startled by the look in his wife's face. Not keep Madeleine! The mere thought of parting with the old woman, whom she had come to regard almost as a second mother, shocked her so much that for a moment she could not formulate a reply.

"But we couldn't get along without her!" she said. "Think of all she does for me and for Jeanne!"

"Oh, Jeanne! It's always Jeanne, Jeanne. I'm sick of hearing her name. If Jeanne hadn't been born we shouldn't be in the pretty box we're in now, and you'd be going on with your work like a sensible woman. I tell you we must economize. We're under heavy expenses here, and we're going to lose a lot of money by this imaginary sickness of yours."

"I can't let Madeleine go," Blanche replied. "I should die without her. I should die of loneliness. And she loves you so, as much as if you were her son, and she loved your mother. She has often talked to me about her. I can't, I can't let her go. I'd rather—"

"Very well, then. Don't say anything more about it. We'll have to economize in some other way. Here she comes now. So keep quiet, or she'll want to find out what we've been talking about."

Chapter XVIII

The Hippodrome was crowded on the night of Miss King's first appearance. Jules, in evening dress as usual, leaned against the railing behind the highest tier of seats. At this moment he felt that he had been duped by fate, and he wanted to revenge himself on the crowd that had come to rejoice over his disappointment; for their presence seemed like a personal insult to him. But for the machinations of that crazy Englishwoman, Blanche would now be going on with her work; by this time they might have made arrangements for her visit to America in the early summer. However, the mischief was done, and there was no knowing when it would be undone. Blanche might have recovered in a few weeks from her terror of the plunge; but after once yielding to it, she would probably never get over it.

Jules believed in presentiments, and he had a strong presentiment that Blanche had taken her plunge for the last time. He tried to console himself, however, with the hope that Lottie King would make a failure. The extensive advertising that Marshall had given her made Jules hate the girl; her name had been posted in places all over London where his wife's alone had been. To Jules this was the most cruel evidence of his own decadence.

Half an hour before it was time for Blanche to appear Jules sauntered toward her dressing-room. When he reached the door, he stopped in surprise; he could hear an unfamiliar voice speaking English. Some one must be in there with Blanche and Madeleine. When he entered, he saw a plump, pretty young woman, with a shock of yellow hair and big blue eyes, dressed in a tight-fitting bathing-suit of blue flannel and in blue silk stockings. He recognized her at once from her photographs.

"Hello!" she cried, glancing at Jules familiarly. "Is this him? Introduce me, won't you?"

For a moment Blanche, whose face had been made up and whose figure, dressed in white silk tights, was covered with the cloak she threw off as she entered the ring, looked confused. Then she presented Jules to Miss King, who beamed upon him with extravagant pleasure.

"Your wife's been telling me about you," she said. "I've been making friends with her. I wanted to see what she was like, and I supposed she'd want to see what I was like. So we've agreed not to scratch each other's eyes out. You speak English too, don't you?"

This gave Jules an opportunity to reiterate his story about having learned English in America.

"So you've been to America!" Miss King cried, her eyes bigger than ever, and her open mouth showing her white, square teeth. "Were you with a troupe there?"

Jules shook his head. "I wasn't married then."

"Ah!" The diver glanced sharply at Blanche, and then back at Jules, as if making a rapid calculation of their ages. "Been married long?" she asked.

"A little over a year," Blanche replied.

"Too bad your wife had to give her dive up, ain't it?" the girl said to Jules. "I hear it was great. But I suppose you'll do it again, won't you, when you're better?"

Blanche flushed. "I don't know," she said, with a half-frightened look at Jules.

"Well, I would if I was you. It's sensational things like that that ketches 'em. My act's kind of sensational, but it ain't in it with yours for cold nerve an' grit. When you do it again you'd oughter go to America. You can make a good deal more there than you do here. I came over just for the reputation. It helps you a lot over there if you've made a hit in Europe."

"But you are English, aren't you?" Jules asked.

"Oh, yes, I s'pose I am, in a sort of way. I was born over here, but my father took me to America when I was about six, an' I'm American to the backbone."

"Have you been in the ring long?" Blanche asked.

"No, I only took to giving performances about five years ago; but I've been in the swimming business all my life. My Dad had a swimming school out in 'Frisco; but there's more money in this business. But I guess I'm keeping you folks. It must be most time for your act. Good-bye. P'raps I'll see you later. I'm mighty glad you can speak English," she laughed, with a glance at Jules. "I travelled with a troupe once with a lot of Italians in it, and my, what a time I had tryin' to talk with 'em!"

She hurried out, leaving Jules with a vision of tousled yellow hair, a roguish smile, and gleaming white teeth, and with the sound of a rich contralto voice in his ears. As soon as the door closed, he turned to Blanche.

"How did she happen to come in here?"

"She wanted me to help her with one of her slippers that was torn. Madeleine sewed it up for her."

"Hasn't she got any maid?"

"She left her behind in Manchester. She was sick. She's coming on when she gets better."

Jules merely grunted and walked out of the room. The sound of the contralto voice was still in his ears. What a sweet voice it was! She seemed to him just like an American in spite of her birth, and Jules preferred the Americans to the English. He wondered what her performance was like, and he waited impatiently for Blanche to finish her act on the trapeze and the rope. As his eyes followed Blanche, he kept seeing the tousled hair and the broad smile revealing the white teeth.

It took several moments for the tank to be arranged for the crowning performance. The audience waited in good-natured patience, however, and when finally the plump little figure in blue flannel ran out, there was a round of applause. Lottie King had added a touch of rouge to either cheek, and she looked very pretty as she ran up the flight of steps leading to the edge of the tank, poised there for a moment with the fingers of both hands touching high in the air, and then dived in a graceful curve into the water. She speedily reappeared, shaking her head and laughing, and struck out for the rope that hung from the platform. This she climbed hand over hand, the water dripping from her figure, and glistening on her face.

Jules, whose eyes had been eagerly following her, was surprised to see that she was going to begin her act with the dive, instead of keeping it for the climax. She seemed to take it very coolly, he thought, as she stood on the swaying platform, rubbing her face with a handkerchief and rearranging one of the sleeves of her costume. Then she steadied the platform, and, an instant later, she was cutting, feet foremost, through the air, her arms by her side and her body rigid. When she reached the water, there was very little splashing, and she speedily reappeared, shaking her head again and displaying her white teeth.

Jules had watched the dive breathlessly, Just as he had watched Blanche's on the night when he first saw her in the *Cirque Parisien*, and now he followed her feats of skill and strength with wonder and fascination. When she remained beneath the surface for more than three minutes he felt as if he himself were stifling, and when she reappeared, calm and smiling, he took a long breath.

He supposed that the rescue of one of the circus hands who fell opportunely into the tank would end the performance; but instead of leaving the ring, Lottie King climbed again to the platform. Surely, Jules thought, she would make a mistake if she repeated that plunge. Instead, however, she swung on the edge, leaped backward into the air, and after several swift turns, fell with a crash into the water. As she swam to the ladder, the band burst into triumphant music, and the audience cheered, and began to climb down from the circular seats and to rush to the spot where she was to make her exit.

Then Jules roused himself. He felt as if he had been in a dream. He had difficulty in reaching Blanche's dressing-room, for the crowd had gathered at the entrance to the ring in order to catch another glimpse of the dripping figure of the diver. When finally he succeeded in making his way there, he found Blanche sitting motionless, her arms resting on the table. He at once divined the cause of her dejection.

"You see what you've brought on yourself," he said. "A lot you'll amount to now! You might as well give up the business."

Madeleine looked at him with mild reproach in her eyes. He paid no attention to her, however. He walked back to the door, and turning, he added: "But you can't stay here all night. I thought you'd be dressed by this time. I'll wait out here for you."

Jules looked anxiously up and down the corridor, but he saw no one. He could hear the noise of the crowd slowly wending out of the Hippodrome, and from the dressing-rooms on either side the buzz of voices. Miss King must have succeeded in making her escape to her room.

Chapter XIX

If Jules had tried, he would have been unable to explain the fascination that Lottie King's performance had for him. In daring it was greatly inferior to his wife's plunge; but the fact that Blanche had lost courage lent her rival's serene indifference to danger an added attractiveness for him.

Every night he watched her with more delight. Besides being plucky and skilful, she was so pretty and so amusing! Jules liked to talk with her in the evening before she made her appearance, and she used to convulse him with laughter by her sallies. She soon fell into the habit of running into Blanche's room to ask Madeleine to do services for her, and toward Blanche she adopted a manner of half-amused patronage. By the end of the first week, Blanche had conceived a great dislike for her. This might have been at least partly due to her discovery of the pleasure which Jules took in the diver's society.

Mrs. Tate had expected that, after ceasing to make her plunge, Blanche would improve in health; but she speedily saw that she was mistaken. One afternoon she called at the hotel in Albemarle Street and found Blanche alone with the little Jeanne; Madeleine had just gone out to do some errands. They had a long talk, during which Blanche was obliged to confess that the pain in her back troubled her just as much as ever, and that she was very unhappy. When Mrs. Tate tried to find out why she was unhappy, she could elicit no satisfactory explanation. As soon as she arrived home that night, she repeated the conversation to her husband.

"Do you suppose the little creature can be mercenary, Percy?" she said. "Do you think she can be sorry she isn't risking her neck every day? I wanted to tell her this morning she ought to be ashamed of herself—she ought to think of her child. Suppose she had been killed! What would have become of the child, *I'd* like to know!"

"That other person has made a hit, I see. They're booming her in the papers. Did she speak of her?"

"Not a word!"

"H'm!"

"What do you mean by that, Percy?"

"Oh, nothing."

"I suppose you think she's jealous of her."

"Jealous?" Tate repeated, lifting his eyes. "You told me yourself that she was jealous before she even saw the other performer."

"Yes, and now she's jealous of her success."

"Oh, *professional* jealousy," he said, throwing back his head. A moment later he added: "There are worse kinds of jealousy than that in the world."

Mrs. Tate looked at him closely, but his eyes were fixed on his plate. For a few moments they did not speak; she was pondering his last remark. They understood each other so well that they often divined each other's thoughts. Now she saw that he did not care to discuss the subject, and she let it drop. She continued to think about it so much, however, that she determined to go to the Hippodrome alone some day, to a *matinée*, and see for herself what Blanche's successor as a star performer was like.

She returned home with a sickly feeling of regret and torturing anticipation; she had not only seen Lottie King, but she had also studied the face of Jules Le Baron, who, unconscious of her gaze, stood within a few yards of her seat. What she had observed in his expression, however, she did not communicate to her husband.

Her visit at the Hippodrome made her resolve to be even kinder to Blanche than she had been; she would take her and the child to drive in the Park two or three times a week,—oftener if she could. Mrs. Tate tried to shake off her forebodings, but for the rest of the day they clung to her, and the next morning she woke with them fresh in mind. So she resolved to drive at once to Albemarle Street. The weather was too dull to take the child out, and she would pass the morning with Blanche and try to cheer her up.

When she reached the hotel she felt relieved to find Blanche in a much better frame of mind than she had been on the occasion of her last call. The pain had left her for a few days, Blanche explained, and she had been greatly encouraged; even Jules had spoken of her improvement; he had been so patient with her, and now she felt ashamed of having been so dispirited. Mrs. Tate went away with a feeling that she had been a fool, that her forebodings were ridiculous.

One night at the end of the week, Tate returned home with the announcement that he was to start for Berlin the next day, to confer with the heads of a banking-house there with regard to the floating of a great loan. He gave her the choice of staying at home or of starting with him after only a few hours of preparation. She chose to start, and for two months she did not see London again; for, once away from the routine of his work, Tate took advantage of the opportunity to run for a holiday from Berlin down to Dresden, and thence over to Paris. During this time Mrs. Tate forgot her self-imposed cares, and gave herself up to the pleasures of travelling.

When she returned home, she was surprised to hear that Madame Le Baron had called several times, and had left word that she was anxious to see her as soon as she came back. This news sent her with a throbbing heart to Albemarle Street; she felt sure that something terrible had happened, something she might have prevented by staying in London. She was always assuming responsibilities and then dropping them! How often her husband had told her that! She had been more than culpable, she kept saying to herself, in going away without even bidding Blanche good-bye, without even leaving an address.

When she arrived at the hotel, at the close of a cold, foggy afternoon, she was surprised to be told by the *garçon* that Madame Le Baron had left, and had gone to an apartment in Upper Bedford Place. "It was too expensive for them here," the *garçon* explained with a contemptuous grin. "So they went to a private house."

Mrs. Tate drove at once to the number the boy gave her, and a few moments later she was climbing the stairs to Blanche's apartment. She was out of breath when she rapped on the door, and still breathing hard when Madeleine admitted her into the shabby drawing-room. A moment later, as Blanche appeared from the next room, she uttered an exclamation.

"Good Heavens, child, what has happened to you! You're whiter than ever, and so *thin*! What have you been doing to yourself? Have you had an illness?"

Blanche shook her head. "No, I haven't been ill," she replied, but her looks and her manner seemed to belie her words. The gray cloth dress which had once fitted her tightly now hung loosely about her; her face was drawn and of a chalklike pallor, and under the eyes were two black lines betraying weeks of suffering and sleeplessness.

"You were thin enough before I went away," said Mrs. Tate, "but now you're a perfect spectre."

Then she went on to explain how she had happened to desert her friends for so long a time. "I know you have something to tell me," she said, starting from her seat, "but before you begin I want to see Jeanne. How is she? But first tell me how you happened to come way up here. Isn't it a long distance for you to climb after your performance every night?"

"Jules chose these rooms because they were so much cheaper than the hotel," Blanche replied simply. "We prepare our own meals, too, and we save in that way. You know my salary is so much smaller than it used to be."

Mrs. Tate made no comment, and they went into the other room, where Jeanne was sleeping in the crib.

"She sleeps nearly all the time," said Blanche, with a faint smile that seemed to exaggerate the expression of pain and weariness in her face.

"How big she's growing!" Mrs. Tate whispered. "There's certainly nothing the matter with *her*, the dear little thing, with her fat rosy cheeks. I'd just like to take her in my arms and hug her."

For several minutes they stood talking about the child; then they left her with Madeleine and went back to the drawing-room, which Mrs. Tate's keen eyes discovered was used also as a bedroom. "They must be economizing with a vengeance," she thought. Blanche closed the door, and took a seat behind her visitor on the couch.

"Now I want to hear all about it," Mrs. Tate cried. "Something has happened. What is it?" She took both of Blanche's hands and looked into her eyes. "What is it?" she repeated.

For a moment they sat looking at each other. Then Blanche bent forward, buried her head on Mrs. Tate's lap, and burst into tears. Mrs. Tate said nothing, and allowed the paroxysm to spend itself. Then, gradually, the story came out.

Jules didn't love her any more, Blanche moaned. He had been cruel to her, oh, so cruel; he had said such dreadful things! And then there had been days and days when he scarcely spoke to her or to the little Jeanne or to Madeleine, and he had grown so strict with them all; he hardly allowed Madeleine enough to buy the things they needed. And once, he had said such dreadful things about Jeanne. He didn't love even Jeanne any more,—poor little Jeanne! He said they would have been better off if she had never been born. Oh, that had nearly killed her, that he should have spoken so about Jeanne. She didn't care so much about herself, though sometimes she wanted to die. One night she had prayed that God would take her and Jeanne together. Jules had always been so good to her until—until that woman came, that woman who had taken her place in the circus. It was that woman who had come between them, with her white teeth and her mocking laugh. She was making a fool of Jules; she did not care for him, but she pretended that she did, just to amuse herself. Jules followed her about everywhere; he even talked of going to America, because she was to go in a few weeks, when her engagement at the Hippodrome was over. But Blanche would die; she would throw herself into the river with Jeanne in her arms rather than go there now. Ah, it had been so hard for her, alone in a strange country, with no one but Madeleine to confide in. Madeleine had been so good; but she, too, had grown afraid of Jules in these last weeks. They scarcely dared to speak when he was at home, now.

From broken utterances, Mrs. Tate pieced together the whole miserable story. For the moment, her pity was lost in admiration for her husband's perspicacity. He had foreseen this! Now, for the first time, she realized what she had vaguely surmised before, the full meaning of his mysterious remark about Blanche and Jules. Then she turned her attention to the prostrate figure before her, offering sympathy and counsel. She knew that she was speaking in platitudes, but they were all she could offer then; and, after all, it was Blanche's own outburst that would do the poor pent-up creature the most good, the consciousness that she had some one to confide in.

Mrs. Tate stayed in the little apartment a long time, and when she went away, Blanche seemed to feel more hopeful. "Act as if he were just as kind to you as ever," was her parting injunction, "and I know everything will come out all right. He'll find out that that dreadful woman is only making a fool of him, and then he'll care more for you than ever."

In her heart, however, Mrs. Tate knew that what she said was not true. Jules had probably grown tired of his wife. The more she thought of the case, the more she pitied Blanche,—the more she realized what a tragedy in the poor little woman's life it meant. And she really had been to blame, she kept saying to herself. But for her interference, Blanche would have gone on with her diving, that other performer would not have come to the Hippodrome, and all of Blanche's agony of jealousy and neglect would have been avoided.

Oh, what a lesson it taught her! Never, *never* would she interfere in a family again! She would have done much better to let Blanche go to her death, rather than to drive her to despair, perhaps to a worse form of death by her meddling.

On reaching home, she was in a fever of remorse and sympathy, and she passed a miserable hour waiting for her husband to return. When at last he did appear, she met him in the hall.

"Percy," she cried dramatically, "you're a prophet!"

"Am I, indeed?" he said, putting his umbrella in the rack. "Do you mean to say this is the first time you've found it out?"

"I'll never doubt your word again, Percy," she went on, stifling a sob. Her appeal to her husband for sympathy threatened to make her hysterical, but she controlled herself and gasped out: "Don't you remember what you said about that man, Le Baron,—you know, the night he dined here, about his falling in love with his wife's performance! Well, that's just what he did do. He didn't fall in love with *her*; he's never *been* in love with her, poor thing. Fortunately she doesn't know that. It's only her *performance*, that horrible plunge she used to make, that he's been in love with all along."

"I don't see anything very prophetic about that," he said, walking into the drawing-room, where she followed him, clutching at the lace handkerchief in her hand. "It was as plain as daylight to any one that heard him talk and saw what kind of man he was."

"I don't mean your seeing merely that. I could tell from what you said that you saw a great deal more. Don't you remember what you said about *professional* jealousy not being the worst kind of jealousy in the world? That was the first thing that opened my eyes. I went to the next *matinée* to see for myself if it could be true, and if I hadn't been an idiot I should have realized it all then. But the next day, just before we left for Berlin, I called on that poor woman, and she seemed so much easier in mind, I thought I must have misunderstood what you meant and been mistaken about that look."

"My dear, I don't quite follow you. Aren't you just a little bit illogical?"

"No, I'm not. I'm perfectly logical. I never was more logical in my life."

"I suppose you mean that the fellow has got tired of his wife, now that she's given up her dive, and he's fallen in love with the other woman."

Mrs. Tate rose tragically from her chair and made a sweeping gesture with her right hand. "With the other woman's *performance*."

Tate looked at her for a moment, with smiling incredulity. "How ridiculous!" he said.

"That's exactly what I said when you told me he had fallen in love with his *wife's* performance. I said it was the most ridiculous thing I'd ever heard in my *life*. I couldn't have believed it if I hadn't observed it with my own eyes. But that afternoon I saw him—he stood near me, leaning against the railing—and I wish you could have seen the expression in his face while that woman was exhibiting herself, especially when she made her horrible dives."

For a moment Tate stood without speaking. Then he said:—

"I'm afraid you're putting a romantic interpretation on a very simple sequence of events. That fellow probably did fall in love with his wife's performance, and incidentally he liked the money that went with it. When she stopped her diving and became an ordinary performer, like thousands of others, she ceased to interest him. Then he looked around for some one else to be interested in, and when the other acrobatic person appeared he was just in the condition to be caught."

"I don't believe it. It's a——"

"There's one way, of course, of proving whether you're right or not," Tate interrupted, with a quizzical smile.

"What's that?"

"If your theory is correct, the only thing for Madame Le Baron to do is to go back to her performance. Then she'll meet her rival on her own ground. From what I've read about that other performer, Madame Le Baron's dive must be twice as difficult and twice as thrilling as hers."

Mrs. Tate turned to her husband with a look of admiration, her breath coming and going in quick gasps. "Percy, that's the wisest thing you've ever said in your life." A moment later she added, with a change of tone: "But isn't the whole thing *too* absurd?"

He started to go upstairs. "You know we're due at the Bigelows in an hour?"

"Wait a minute," said Mrs. Tate. "I want to think over what you said. You can't imagine how this thing has worried me. It's all due to my meddling. Oh, I know that; you needn't say anything to me about it. But I'm determined to help that poor woman if I can. Oh, if I had only followed your advice, and let them alone!" she moaned.

"There's no use worrying now. The mischief's done. He would probably have got tired of her anyway."

"If something isn't done to bring him back to her," she went on without heeding his remark, "it will kill her. I'm sure of that. If you could only see her. She looks like a ghost, and her hands tremble so! I don't believe she's slept a wink for weeks. I don't see how she gets through her performances. A clinging creature like her just *lives* on affection. Before she was married she always had her mother to take care of her. To think that that man should treat her so! Oh, it's a shame, it's a shame!"

Tate was standing at the door. "If she's going to kill herself over that fellow, she might as well have gone on with her diving and killed herself that way. You ask her if she doesn't want to go back to it," he added, with the quizzical smile, "and see if she won't jump at the chance."

"Do you suppose that she can suspect for an instant that her husband fell in love with her performance?" she said, her eyes following her husband up the stairs.

"She probably hasn't reasoned it out, but I haven't a doubt she feels it intuitively," he replied, continuing his ascent. "You just ask her if she doesn't want to make the plunge again and see what she'll say," he concluded, smiling down at her from the floor above.

Chapter XX

Mrs. Tate tried, by an almost impassioned kindness, to atone for her neglect of Blanche during her absence from London. She sent her flowers from her conservatory, she bought gifts for the little Jeanne, she called at the apartment in Upper Bedford Place nearly every morning. During these visits she did not once meet Jules; Blanche told her that he always went away soon after breakfast, and seldom returned before dinner. Sometimes he did not accompany her to the Hippodrome, but he never failed to appear there during the evening. The management had offered to reëngage Miss King as soon as her contract expired, and the diver thought of postponing her return to America; but they had not as yet come to terms, as the girl wanted a much larger salary than she had been receiving.

It was this information that reminded Mrs. Tate to ask Blanche if she were sorry she had given up her plunge and if she ever wished to resume it. Though she had at first been impressed by the solution of Blanche's troubles suggested by her husband, she had on sober second thought dismissed it as ridiculously romantic; such things might happen in novels, but they never could occur in real life. Her belief was shaken, however, when she saw the pale face light up at her question.

"Oh, yes," Blanche cried, "I have thought of it. Sometimes—sometimes I think it would be better if I hadn't given it up. Then—then that woman wouldn't have come." Her eyes filled with tears, but she controlled herself and, a moment later, she went on:—

"But I—I thought it was wrong for me to risk my life, and it made me so unhappy for Jeanne's sake. But sometimes I think I might have stopped being afraid. Before Jeanne was born I never had the least thought of fear, even after father was killed, because I knew that was because the trapeze was weak. Oh, I'm sure," she went on piteously,—"I'm *sure* I shouldn't be afraid any more!"

"But Dr. Broughton, you remember what he said, don't you?"

"He said that when I stopped making the plunge I should be better," Blanche replied simply. "But I'm not better; I feel worse,—oh, so much worse! I know I should be better if I tried it again. And I sha'n't be afraid any more," she repeated,—"even for Jeanne. It would be so much better for us all!"

This speech made Mrs. Tate wonder if, as her husband had suggested, Blanche had divined that Jules had cared for her performance rather than for herself, and fancied she could win him back by resuming it. Her interest increased when she learned that Jules and Miss King had not spoken to each other for two evenings. Miss King's maid, who had at last come from Manchester, and who knew a little Canadian French, had told Madeleine about it. Jules had urged Miss King to accept Marshall's terms, and was vexed with her because she refused and threatened to go back to America. This had made him even more disagreeable at home than he had been before; for the past few days he had not spoken one pleasant word to them, and he had not even noticed Jeanne.

It was this information that rang in Mrs. Tate's consciousness when she had left the apartment. Jules and that woman had quarrelled! Of course, they would make it up again,—perhaps in a few days, perhaps that very day; but if they did not, the quarrel might be one of the means of winning him back to his wife. At any rate, she would speak to her husband about it. When, on her return home, she did speak, he burst out laughing.

"I don't see how you can find anything funny in that!" she said resentfully. "It's a very serious matter."

"But it threatens to spoil my beautiful little romance!"

"Your beautiful romance? What do you mean?"

"If you had persuaded her to go back to her diving, and if she drove the other woman out of the field in that way, it would be a proof of my theory that he's fallen in love with the *performance* and not with the *performer*. But if his wife gets him back again now, it will be merely because the other woman has broken with him. There's nothing for him to do *except* to go back to his wife and be forgiven."

"Well, I don't care what the reason is—if she only *gets* him back. She'll certainly die of jealousy and misery if she doesn't,—that's plain enough. In my opinion, Dr. Broughton was entirely wrong in his diagnosis of the case. She says herself that she misses her diving and she wants to take it up again. Her rest hasn't done her a particle of good. Anyway, I'll speak to the Doctor about it to-morrow. I'll write a note, and ask him to come in for tea if he can."

"And hold another council of war," her husband suggested.

"A council of *peace*," she retorted smartly. "Oh, I know what you're thinking of! But I'm determined to undo the harm I've done. There's no time to be lost. If I can get that poor little woman to resume her plunge while the husband's still quarrelling with the other performer, I feel sure everything will come out all right. He'll be interested in her again. Don't you remember how he used to brag about her? I suppose you don't, but he did; and I could tell that he was as proud of her as if she were the most wonderful creature in the world."

"I don't see what she wants him for," Tate said carelessly.

"Well, you're not a woman, and you can't understand how women feel about men. I sometimes think the worse men are, the more their wives adore them."

Tate smiled, but he made no reply; he was much more interested in the case than he would allow himself to appear to be. Indeed, he was so interested that he left his office the next day earlier than usual, in order to take part in the conference. He found his wife in earnest talk with the Doctor. Before coming to the house, Dr. Broughton, at Mrs. Tate's suggestion, had made a call on Madame Le Baron, and he expressed his alarm at having found her so thin and weak.

"Do you remember what I said the night we had our first talk about her?" he asked, glancing at Tate. "I was afraid then that if she gave up her work it might upset her, though I didn't see how she could go on with the diving and keep whatever health she had. Now she's a great deal worse off than she was when I last saw her."

Then they discussed the case in all its aspects. The Doctor laughed when Mrs. Tate declared she believed the poor woman's happiness depended on her resuming her plunge. "Oh, it may seem absurd to you!" she cried, growing more earnest under ridicule; "but Percy believes it, though he may pretend to you that he doesn't. He was the one who first suggested it to me."

"I really think the diving wouldn't hurt her health so much as her worrying about her husband does," the Doctor admitted. "Besides, she believes she won't be afraid of it any more. She says her rest from it has taken all her fear away."

"Then you think the best thing for her to do would be to resume the plunge?" said Mrs. Tate.

For a moment the Doctor stroked his chin. "Under the circumstances I should say it might," he replied slowly. "At any rate, it would be worth trying. Of course, if that haunting fear returned she'd have to stop it again."

A look of triumph flashed from the face of Mrs. Tate; and when she glanced at her husband she saw that he was trying to dissemble his interest in the decision. "I shall tell her that to-morrow!" she cried. "It'll be the best news the poor thing has had for a long time. She's crazy to begin that plunge again."

"I hope you are ready to take the consequences of your interference in this business," said Tate, dryly.

Chapter XXI

The next morning, in a long and secret talk, Mrs. Tate communicated the Doctor's judgment to Blanche. She learned that Jules was still sullen and depressed. That, of course, was a sign that his quarrel with the diver had not as yet been made up. Blanche said that she would speak to him at once about resuming the plunge; so far as she knew, no one had as yet been engaged to take Miss King's place, and perhaps Mr. Marshall would make a new contract with her on the old terms. Mrs. Tate hurried away in a state of feverish excitement, dreading, yet hoping, that she might meet Jules on the stairs, in order to reveal the great news. She would have liked to return to the apartment that very afternoon, to learn the effect of the announcement upon him; but she controlled her impatience.

Jules did not return till late in the afternoon. From his manner Blanche saw at once that he was in a surly mood. He flung his coat and hat on a chair and threw himself on the couch. For a long time she did not dare to speak to him. She thought he was going to sleep, but she suddenly saw him staring at her with a look that frightened her.

"Jules!" she said.

He had closed his eyes again, and he seemed not to hear.

"Jules."

He opened his eyes, and once more she met that look. "What is it?" he grunted. Her plaintive manner vexed him; it seemed like a reflection on himself.

"There's something I want to say to you," she went on apologetically, and with a suggestion of tearfulness in her voice, as if she felt disappointed at his manner of receiving her news.

As he did not reply, she said: "It's about—about my plunge. I have been thinking that I'm—I'm so much better now—I mean I'm not so nervous—perhaps I can begin it again."

He sat up on the couch, a light coming into his eyes. For a moment he was too surprised to speak. Then he said: "Well, I'm glad you're coming to your senses!"

Encouraged by the change in his manner, she repeated what Dr. Broughton had said to Mrs. Tate. At the mention of the names, Jules' face darkened; since that night at the Tates' he had felt a personal resentment against the Doctor, almost as strong as his hatred of the Englishwoman.

"So that woman's been here again today, has she?" he said bitterly. After a brief silence, he added more gently: "If you feel able to do the plunge again, the sooner you begin the better. I know that Marshall will be glad enough to renew the old contract. It will just fit in with his plans," he continued, with a grim thought of the diver's discomfiture on being superseded by Blanche. "I'll speak to him this very night."

Blanche tried to smile, but the effort ended in a sigh. She had thought that Jules would show more enthusiasm.

"But we can't have any more nonsense," he said, glancing at her again,—this time, however, without the bitterness she had before observed in his face. "If you allow yourself to be afraid of the plunge again, it will simply ruin you as an attraction. It'll make the managers think you're unreliable, and they won't engage you."

In spite of his apparent indifference, Jules was secretly delighted at the thought of his wife's resuming her great dive. For the past few days he had never felt so keenly the humiliation of his own position. A petulant remark of Lottie King's the day of their quarrel had kept ringing in his ears: "What do *you* amount to anyway?" Now he thought triumphantly of the restoration of his own dignity. With Blanche as the star attraction of the Hippodrome, earning a large salary, and with a choice of offers from all over the world, he would become a personage again! But he must guard her more carefully. He must in future keep her out of the way of interfering foreigners like Mrs. Tate, who would put a lot of nonsense into her head!

That night, when Jules consulted Marshall, he learned what he had already surmised, that the manager was much upset by Miss King's refusal to extend her engagement on any but exorbitant terms, and though it would be completed in two weeks, he had not as yet found a sufficiently strong attraction to take her place; so he was not only willing, but glad, to renew with Blanche the contract she had at first made with him. Jules felt the more elated on being told that Miss King had not been nearly so good an attraction as his wife while giving the sensational plunge. He was in high spirits when he entered Blanche's dressing-room and told her the news. Blanche flushed with pleasure, not merely at the news, but at his affectionate manner as well; Madeleine, however, though she said nothing, seemed depressed. She had hoped that the poor child would never make that horrible dive again.

After that night Blanche was so happy that she seemed like another creature from the thin, white-faced little woman of the past few weeks. Her eyes were bright, her cheeks flushed. Jules had been so different with her, she said to Mrs. Tate, since she had told him she would go on with the plunge. The night before he had taken her to the Hippodrome, and after the performance they had gone with Madeleine to a *café*; it reminded them of the days of their courtship in Paris.

The two weeks that followed were the happiest Blanche had known since those first days after the birth of her child. Jules' devotion extended not only to her, but to little Jeanne and to Madeleine as well. For several days the gloom that had wrapped the city during most of the winter lifted; the sun shone, and the feeling of spring was in the air. In the afternoons Blanche took walks with Jules in the park, and on Sunday they went to mass together and then drove out to Richmond and dined there. They agreed to pretend that they were still in their days of courtship, and Jules delighted Blanche by repeating some of the foolish speeches he had made to her in the first weeks of their love.

Then, too, they made great plans for the future. The negotiations with Hicks in New York had been broken off, but Jules had heard of an Australian manager who was in London looking for performers to appear during the following winter in Melbourne. How fine it would be if they could go out there and give performances in the chief Australian cities! Blanche, however, showed so little enthusiasm for this plan that Jules abandoned it for a time. Besides, he himself liked better the plan she suggested of returning to the *Cirque Parisien*. They might make an engagement there that would enable them to pass the winter in Paris. How good it would be to be back there again! Perhaps they could secure the little apartment in the *rue de Lisbonne*. Jules became so enthusiastic that he wrote to the manager in Paris, proposing terms. After a winter there they might think of going to Australia, where they would be much better paid than in Paris.

The thought of returning to France added to Blanche's happiness. Oh, to see her mother and Jeanne and Louise again! How good it would be! There had been times during the past few weeks when she felt as if she could not bear to be separated from them any longer. But in Paris they could come to see her; perhaps Monsieur Berthier would let her mother and the girls pass a few weeks with her. Of course, she would be with them in Boulogne for the summer. When she spoke of this to Jules, however, he said nothing. He had in mind other plans, a possible engagement at one of the French watering places; but he thought it best not to refer to this at present. He realized the importance of making as much money as possible and as quickly as possible. There was no knowing how long his wife's nerve would last. If she only held out for a few years longer, they could make a fortune in Australia and America. Then they could retire, and live comfortably in Paris for the rest of their lives. He expected to earn a great deal of money in

America; but he had reasons for not speaking of that country at all for the present.

The two weeks during which Blanche was enjoying her new happiness were an exciting time for Mrs. Tate, who felt as if she were responsible for the success of her *protégée's* return to her former place in the Hippodrome. Every day she repaired to Upper Bedford Place and held long conferences with Blanche. Everything promised well, she thought. Jules showed no signs of returning to the thraldom of Lottie King. How providential, Mrs. Tate thought, the quarrel between them had been! She did not know that, even before his break with her, Jules had begun to tire of the diver's domineering manner and of her habit of ridiculing him; moreover, he had at last perceived that she was only playing with him. This had helped to prejudice him against her performance, and as the novelty of the performance wore off, he saw that it was far inferior in daring and skill to his wife's magnificent plunge. This had never lost its fascination for him, and now, as he assisted Blanche in her daily exercises he felt the old thrill at its brilliancy and his own sense of importance in having a part in it.

On the afternoon of the day when her plunge was to be resumed, Blanche took a long rest. She was awakened by the crowing of Jeanne in the next room. She raised her hands to her head; at the thought of the ordeal of the evening, a sudden dizziness came upon her. It was more than three months since she had made the dive, and she wondered if she should be equal to it. How horrible if at the last moment she should lose her nerve! She arose quickly, hardly daring to allow herself to think, and she hurried to the child. How strong and beautiful Jeanne was! Blanche took her in her arms and pressed her closely. When Madeleine turned and lumbered out of the room, leaving them alone together, Blanche began to kiss the child passionately, and tears welled over on her cheeks. Then she bathed her face, for fear that Jules would see that she had been crying.

That night at dinner, Jules was in high spirits. "Marshall expects a big house," he said. "He's spent a lot of money advertising your dive. He thinks of getting a big poster made of you flying through the air."

During the whole of the meal Blanche was very quiet. Madeleine noticed that her eyes were shining. When it was time to go to the Hippodrome, Jules, wrapping his wife in her cloak, put his arms around her, and kissed her on the ear, as he had often done in the days of their engagement. She drew away and started for Jeanne's room.

"Where are you going?" he said.

"I want to kiss the little one good-night."

"But she's asleep!" he cried impatiently. "You mustn't wake her up."

In spite of his protest, she silently made her way into the room where the child lay, closing the door behind her. Jules listened, thinking that Jeanne would cry on being disturbed; but there was no sound. Then he knew that she was praying by the crib, and this angered him. It was about time to put a stop to her notions, he said to himself. When, a moment later, she came out, her face was covered with a thick veil, and, after glancing at her sharply, he said nothing.

On arriving at the Hippodrome, they found Mrs. Tate in the star dressing-room, which had been assigned to Blanche again.

"I have been waiting for you," Mrs. Tate said nervously. "I suppose I have no right to be here, but I felt that I *must* see you, and I made my husband bring me. Are you quite well?"

She had observed the look of disgust given her by Jules, but this did not disturb her nearly so much as the white face that Blanche presented. Moreover, she did not feel reassured when Blanche smiled and said she felt perfectly well.

"Of course everything will be splendid. There's a tremendous crowd," Mrs. Tate added. "You'll have a great success."

Jules, after bowing coldly, had turned from the room. As soon as the door closed behind him, Mrs. Tate seized Blanche by both hands and kissed her affectionately. "I mustn't keep you from dressing," she said with a smile. "Perhaps I'll come in and congratulate you when it's all over."

Blanche grew a shade paler, and Mrs. Tate hesitated at the door. "What is it?" she said.

"Nothing."

Mrs. Tate walked toward her. "Nothing?"

Blanche turned her head away. "If anything should happen," she said quietly, "the—the little one—I should like my mother to take her."

Mrs. Tate began to breathe hard; but she burst out laughing. "You silly child! Of course; I shall look after Jeanne anyway. Don't you worry about *her*. Now I must hurry out to that husband of mine. He'll be furious with me for keeping him waiting so long."

A few moments before Blanche appeared in the ring, Jules returned to the dressing-room, resplendent in his evening clothes, with three diamonds gleaming on his shirt-front, and carrying a bouquet of white roses.

"These are just like the roses I bought for you the night I met you. I selected them this afternoon, and they've just come. You must wear them in your belt, as you did then," he said, as she flushed with pleasure and thanked him. "I remember how tickled I was when I saw them; and oh, how

I hated Pelletier when you took them out and gave them to him to hold, while you were going through your act."

Then, as she adjusted the flowers in her belt, he went on: "It's the biggest house of the season! Marshall says you're the best attraction he ever had. Ready?" he asked, surveying Blanche as she stood in her white silk tights. "You look just as you did when I first saw you," he added, putting one hand on her cheek and kissing her lightly on the other. "Come along."

Then he threw over her the robe she always wore on her way to the ring, and they hurried from the room. As Blanche ran out on the net and heard the applause of the vast audience, she felt a thrill of joy and an intoxicating sense of her own power. All fear seemed to leave her, and she laughed as she climbed hand over hand to the trapeze. From trapeze to trapeze she shot with delight; she had never felt so sure of herself, so exultant. When she returned to the net, Jules, who had taken his place at the rope, whispered to her: "You're in great form to-night. Keep it up."

She was smiling as she started on her long climb to the top of the building. But when she had taken her place on the beam from which she was to make her plunge and looked down at the black mass in the distance, her strength seemed suddenly to leave her. Her fingers tightened on the beam, as if she felt afraid of losing her balance. Then she heard her husband's voice ring through the place, crying the familiar warning. She knew the moment had come for making the plunge; but she continued motionless. She felt as if her will had become suddenly paralyzed, and a moment later, as if her body were frozen.

The black mass below seemed to dance before her, then to beckon to her, and in her ears she kept hearing the voice of little Jeanne and the sound of her laughter. Oh, she had known that this moment would come some time; she had known it ever since Jeanne was born. But she could not sit there forever; the crowd below was waiting to see her fall. If she did not make an effort she should lose her self-control and go plunging into the blackness. She must lift her hands and gather herself together, and hurl herself out as she had always done. But she had no strength; she could only lift her arms weakly. Then she tried to give her body the necessary impetus, and she plunged wildly into the air.

There was a cry of horror from the crowd, and a moment later the white figure lay motionless in the net. The people rose from their seats and rushed toward the ring. The police tried to drive them back as Jules leaped into the net and seized the prostrate body in his arms.

"Keep them back," he cried frantically, not realizing that he was speaking French. "She must have air." Then, turning, he said: "Blanche! Blanche! Can't you speak? Open your eyes so I may know you aren't dead."

He was terrified by the way her head fell back from her shoulders. "We must get her out of this," he said desperately, to two of the circus men who had followed him on the net, as he glanced down at the struggling mass beneath him. "Bring her to her dressing-room. Make those people get out of the way."

With difficulty they bore her through the crowd. Some one threw her cloak over her as she passed. She gave no sign of life, but the expression in Jules' face showed that he still hoped. When they reached her room, they placed her on the floor, and Jules closed the door to keep out the crowd. Madeleine, who had been ringing her hands and moaning, quickly loosened the tight bodice. Then the door was forced open again, and Marshall entered with a physician, who quickly bent over the prostrate figure and listened for the heart-beat.

"She's dead," he said quietly.

Jules threw himself on the body in a paroxysm of despair.